THE MURDER OF DIANA DEVON

And Other Mysteries

Michael Gilbert
Edited and Introduced by
John Cooper

CHIVERS

British Library Cataloguing in Publication Data available

This Large Print edition published by BBC Audiobooks Ltd, Bath, 2010.
Published by arrangement with Robert Hale Ltd.

U.K. Hardcover ISBN 978 1 408 49273 4
U.K. Softcover ISBN 978 1 408 49274 1

Printed and bound in Great Britain by CPI Antony Rowe, Chippenham
and Eastbourne

CONTENTS

Introduction 1

The Murder of Diana Devon 10
The Rules of the Game 52
Good Old Monty 75
No Place Like Home 95
St Ethelburga and the Angel of Death 102
The Great German Spy Hunt 144
The Killing of Karl Carver 153
Close Contact 168
The Fire-Raisers 174
Y Mynyddoed Sanctiaidd 201
The Klagenfurt Tote 212
Churchill's Men 221
Coronation Year 262
The Seventh Paragraph 278
Superintendent Mahood and the
    Craven Case 284
Arnold or the Uses of Electricity 311

Appendix 315

INTRODUCTION

Michael Gilbert (1912–2006) was one of the greatest crime writers to emerge after World War II. He received the Crime Writers' Association's highest award, the Cartier Diamond Dagger, for an outstanding contribution to the genre of crime fiction. Both the Mystery Writers of America and the Swedish Academy of Detection honoured him as a Grand Master.

Michael Gilbert wrote 30 novels and 185 short stories, all of which have been collected in fourteen volumes. His novels and stories are always plausible, civilised and entertaining. He was a master of a variety of styles, equally at home writing espionage, thrillers, police procedural and classic detection. Examples of some of his particularly fine novels are *Smallbone Deceased*, *Death Has Deep Roots*, *Death in Captivity* (U.S. *Danger Within*), *The Night of the Twelfth*, *Death of a Favourite Girl* (U.S. *The Killing of Katie Steelstock*) and *The Black Seraphim*. He also wrote plays for radio, television and the stage.

This book contains the eleven remaining previously uncollected stories by Michael Gilbert, dating between 1956 and 1991 as well as two radio plays and a poem. All the stories

1

have appeared only once before. They were originally printed in a wide variety of newspapers, anthologies and magazines. In addition, there are two previously unpublished stories, *The Fire-Raisers* and *Y Mynyddoed Sanctiaidd*.

During his long career as a writer, Gilbert wrote three competition stories, all of which are whodunits. The first, *The Murder of Diana Devon*, originally titled *Can you Solve A Murder?*, was published in the *Daily Express* between 21 and 26 May, 1956. Readers were encouraged to 'be your own detective' and to try to spot the killer before the Saturday's issue when the murderer was revealed. This story introduced 'Superintendent Mahood head of all C.I.D. in that division, who looked like a carrion crow in a bowler hat'.

The Rigby File, published in 1989 by Hodder and Stoughton, consists of fictional incidents in the life of a female spy, Dorothy Mayotte Rigby. A team of thirteen distinguished crime writers each contributed a chapter of the story about Dorothy Rigby, with a connecting account by Tim Heald. Michael Gilbert wrote *The Rules of the Game*, 'in which Rigby holds a *réunion dangereuse* in Occupied France'.

Hilary Hale edited several editions of *Winter's Crimes*, an annual anthology which was first published in 1969 by Macmillan and ran for twenty-four years. Gilbert provided four stories to this excellent series. In 1991,

Hilary Hale became the editor of *Midwinter Mysteries I*, published by Scribners, for which Michael Gilbert composed 'Good Old Monty'. There were five volumes in this short series with Gilbert contributing to three of them.

During the 1950s and 1960s, the *London Evening Standard* newspaper had a long running series entitled 'Did It Happen?'. Whether the story was actually true or fiction was then revealed the following day. Michael Gilbert provided three tales for the series: The fictional *No Place Like Home* on 3 August 1957 and two true stories, *The Seventh Paragraph* on 9 October 1957 and *Close Contact* on 15 December 1960. The last mentioned appeared in the newspaper as *Face To Face With A Burglar—Was I Wrong to Help Him?* even though Gilbert's preferred title was the more subtle *Close Contact* to which I have reverted.

Over a period of thirty years, Michael Gilbert wrote several plays for the radio. During 1968 and 1969, he wrote a series of plays for BBC radio which was broadcast in twenty episodes under the title *Game Without Rules*, (see appendix). Some of the plays were broadcast over two nights. All of the plays feature Mr Daniel Joseph Calder and Mr Samuel Behrens who are ruthless and efficient counter-intelligence agents recruited by MI6 in the 1930s. Their controller is Mr

Fortescue, seemingly the manager of the Westminster branch of the London and Home Counties Bank. To him, the word liquidation most certainly had two meanings. When he wished to make contact with Mr Calder or Mr Behrens he would convey a message to them that their accounts were causing him concern. Calder's Persian deerhound, Rasselas, assists in some of their investigations.

Five of the plays were based on stories in the collection *Game Without Rules* 1967 (US), 1968 (UK). Another eight have parallels with stories collected in the 1982 title *Mr Calder and Mr Behrens*. Whilst one play, *Double, Double*, is similar to the story published in *Even Murderers Take Holidays* in 2007.

Importantly, two of the plays, *Churchill's Men* and *St Ethelburga and the Angel of Death*, were written especially for radio, and here these scripts have their first publication. In *Churchill's Men*, Calder and Behrens try to prevent revelations in a court case being made public which could jeopardise a British double agent. *St Ethelburga and the Angel of Death* involves the search for a Nazi war criminal amongst the staff of an English boys' prep. school.

Mr Calder was played by Stephen Murray, Mr Behrens by Peter Howell and Mr Fortescue by Carleton Hobbs (who notably played Sherlock Holmes in over seventy radio adaptations). Both plays were produced by

David H. Godfrey.

Lilliput was originally a small format monthly magazine and was first issued in July 1937. Later it increased in size and ran until 1960. During the late 1950s, Michael Gilbert wrote four stories for the magazine. Two of these stories have already been collected. In this volume, *The Klagenfurt Tote*, (September 1956) is a carefree second world war anecdote, being no.7 in a series called 'Where The Fighting Was Thinnest'. *The Great German Spy Hunt* (March 1958) was the first story in a new series where writers were asked to recall incidents from their scholastic past.

The television programme *Whodunnit?* was a panel game on ITV devised by Lance Percival and Jeremy Lloyd. On 28 June 1976, a new seven part series of this solve it yourself detective programme was due to start. In anticipation of this, Michael Gilbert wrote *The Killing of Karl Carver* (originally titled *Who Killed Karl Carver?*) which was printed in the TV Times of 15 April 1976 as a competition story. Readers were invited to send in their solutions to the murder story to win the opportunity to become panelists on the show.

Fifteen contestants with the correct solution and convincing explanations of the crime were then invited to Thames Television Studios to take part in an audition. Their ability to cross-examine was tested and their deductive powers assessed by Percival, Lloyd and the chairman of the panel, Jon Pertwee. Seven lucky viewers were then chosen and each would appear in one of the seven episodes alongside celebrities such as Sheila Hancock, Stratford Johns and George Savalas. The team did their best to work out the motive, method and means behind that week's crime story. The prize for the member of the public on the panel was an object from the scene of the crime to take home as a souvenir.

In 1995, Michael Gilbert started what would be his last series of stories, centred around the partnership of Fearne and Bracknell solicitors. Their practice was situated near the northern end of Tower Bridge. Some of the stories had their first appearance in the *Ellery Queen Mystery Magazine*. In 2000, fourteen of the stories were collected in *The Mathematics of Murder*, published by Robert Hale.

The two senior partners are Francis Fearne and Robert Bracknell and the firm, which has a fine reputation, is often affectionately referred to as Fern and Bracken. It is Francis's daughter Tara and Hugo, Robert's son, along with the canny Horace Piggin (Piggy), their managing clerk, who are the operative side of the firm. Although not criminal lawyers, they deal with cases involving arson, blackmail, embezzlement and murder. *The Fire-Raisers*, Fearne and

Bracknell's fifteenth case, was written in the 1990s and has its first publication in this book.

During the 1980s, Michael Gilbert wrote *Y Mynyddoed Sanctiaidd* (The Holy Mountains) under the pseudonym Justus and it is published here for the first time.

Who Done It?, edited by Alice Laurence and Isaac Asimov and published in 1980 in the U.S. by Houghton Mifflin Company, is a most unusual anthology. Not only has the reader to guess 'who done it' but also has then to guess who wrote it. In his forward on style, Isaac Asimov says 'Each writer writes in his or her own style, and it is up to you to spot that style if you can'. The book contains seventeen uncredited stories and a list of the seventeen authors in alphabetical order. The reader must place each story, with the correct author. In the preface to Michael Gilbert's story *Coronation Year*, Isaac Asimov states there is 'Nothing like a multiple mystery, and they don't come more multiple than this. See if you can guess as soon as possible (1) the year, (2) who Teddy was, and (3) the nationality, real name and identity of the lodger. The lodger makes an unlikely hero, but actually I don't think he was ever in Britain.'

In August 1958, The Amalgamated Press Limited published their first volume of *Suspense*, a pocket sized, monthly magazine. Contributors to this first issue included Michael Gilbert, Agatha Christie, Margery

7

Allingham and Georgette Heyer. Gilbert went on to write three other stories for *Suspense*, including a competition story *The Craven Case*, (June 1959). For this volume, the story has been retitled *Superintendent Mahood and the Craven Case*, to avoid confusion with a different story featuring the solicitor, Henry Bohun but with the same title, collected in *The Man Who Hated Banks*.

Readers were invited to 'Catch the Killer' and the entries were judged by Agatha Christie, H.E. Bates, Jack Warner, Fabian of the Yard and the Editor of Suspense. This story was the final investigation for the tenacious Superintendent Mahood. Later Fleetway Publications Ltd. took over publication of *Suspense*. In total, there were thirty-two issues, the last being April 1961. It then merged with its companion magazine *Argosy*. Michael Gilbert had sixty-three stories published in *Argosy*, the first being *The Seventh Musket*, in August 1954, and the last *The Decline and Fall of Mr Behrens*, in January 1973.

Michael Gilbert's light-hearted poem *Arnold or the Uses of Electricity* was included in *Julian Symons At 80—A Tribute*, published by Eurographica in 1000 numbered copies, in 1992. The book was edited by Patricia Craig, and various celebrated crime writers, including Elizabeth Ferrars, Patricia

Highsmith, Reginald Hill and H.R.F. Keating, contributed to honour Julian Symons's 80th birthday.

I would like to thank Barry Pike as well as the staff of the BBC Written Archives for their help in providing information on the radio plays. Barry Pike also kindly supplied copies of the two unpublished stories.

All the known uncollected stories of Michael Gilbert have now been collected in book form. I appreciate the enthusiasm that John Hale has shown for this inestimable author and I am grateful that Robert Hale Ltd. has published so many of the stories.

John Cooper
Westcliff-on-Sea

THE MURDER OF DIANA DEVON

'We were having an argument,' said Ron, 'about mixer-what's-its-name?'

'Rabbit disease.'

'Right. Well, I said to Len, "that's where I saw a rabbit when I was coming off shift yesterday evening." And he called me a liar. Only quite friendly, see.'

'What I said was,' said Len, 'I haven't seen a rabbit in Helenwood for two years, not outside of a hutch.'

'All right,' said Sergeant Butt. 'I got that bit. You were proceeding to your work at the Junction Station. Walking along the embanked portion of the railway line where it traverses Helenwood Common and conversing with Leonard Frampkin on the permanent way staff with yourself.'

'Did I say that?'

'More or less,' said Sergeant Butt. 'I just put it into English for you. What's next?'

'Well, we got to this place and stopped so I could show Len where I saw the rabbit. You can look right down the embankment if you stand on the platform behind the sand-box— and blimey! It was a shoe—with a foot in it. A girl.'

'You perceived a female body lying at the bottom of the embankment.'

10

'Right. Len wanted to go on and report it. But I said no, she mayn't be dead. We gotter look. So we slid down the embankment and when I say slid, I mean slid. It hadn't long stopped raining and it was pretty wet. We got through the wire fence—that's half way up the embankment—and got down to her. She was dead alright.' 'You didn't touch her?'

'Not half we didn't. We got back on to the line and went for the phone. There's one in the signal box.'

'You made your way to the nearest telephone and communicated with the police.'

'Right.'

'Then if you'll kindly put your full names and addresses at the foot of the page that will be all for the moment.'

'What do you mean for the moment. *We* never done nothing.'

'You may be required to attend the inquest as witnesses.'

'Inquest, eh? Some funny business.'

'I didn't say so,' said the sergeant repressively. 'But even if it was an accident there'll be an inquest.'

'Chap they ought to have an inquest on,' said Len, 'is the one who put the fence on the railway side of the cutting. If they'd put it along the top of the other side, people wouldn't go falling into it and breaking their necks. It's a nasty place. There was a kid fell into it the other day and broke his leg—.'

11

'Save it for the coroner,' said Sergeant Butt.

*   *   *

Superintendent Mahood, head of all C.I.D. work in that division, who looked like a carrion crow in a bowler hat, was saying much the same sort of thing to his principal assistant Detective Sergeant Leavis, who looked like a choir-boy but was actually an exceptionally tough young man.

'If only the railway had listened to us last time,' said Mahood, 'and moved the fence back on to the open side of the cutting, this wouldn't have happened. But they didn't want the responsibility of an extra bit of ground and the corporation didn't want to give it up and now they've got a dead body on their hands.'

'Accident, sir?'

'I should think so. Girl's strange to the district. Comes along that path in the dark. Path swings away from the cutting edge. She doesn't notice it and comes right on over the rough. Nothing to stop her. Down she goes.'

'Even in the dark,' said the sergeant, 'she'd know she wasn't on the path. It's 20 yards of grass and quite a bit of scrub before she comes to the edge.'

'All right. She knew she was off the path. And was trying to find her way back. And it was raining in torrents. That can't have helped her. Here comes the medico.'

The pathologist was a thin amiable-looking man, with a third-year undergraduate air, who looked a lot younger than he was. His secretary, a handsome brunette, trotted behind him like an intelligent gun-dog.

'What have you got for us this morning, Superintendent?' he said.

'Just a young lady who's taken a toss. This way. It's a bit steep. Down there. You can't really see her from this side because of the bushes. A rail-man spotted her. He was walking along the line on his way to work. Bit of a fluke he saw her. Something to do with rabbits.'

'If I were a rabbit,' said the pathologist fretfully, 'I expect I could hop down there too. It's pretty wet isn't it? Have you got my galoshes, Milly?'

The secretary opened the case and produced the galoshes. Also a big torch and a pair of gloves.

'Good girl,' said the pathologist. 'Better not come any nearer. Don't want too many footprints. I'll go down a bit further along and work my way back.'

He lowered himself cautiously, clinging to the bushes. They heard his voice booming up.

'Pretty girl. Not long dead. Sporting type. Hiker, perhaps. Wearing macintosh, trousers and sweater, ankle socks and walking shoes.' The girl wrote steadily. The silence was

13

broken only by the pathologist humming to himself.

Presently the voice said, 'Milly, you'll have to come down here. Go the way I came and try not to tread on anything that matters.'

'It's the clothes,' said the pathologist. 'I'm not much good at this sort of thing. What sort of girl do they make her out to be?'

Milly considered them carefully. The transparent macintosh. The brown shoes, good but not hand made. The gaudy ankle socks. The blue serge trousers, the cable-stitch square-fronted sweater with the new scarf, with yellow dogs' heads tucked in neatly round the neck. Then she looked at the hands, taking particular note of the nails, and the make-up, and the hair.

'I'd say,' she said, 'that she was a nice, respectable, middle-class girl. Unmarried but with a job that brought in good money most of which she spent on keeping herself nice. Her perm cost her a few guineas and it wasn't done long ago. And she either went to a manicurist or did her own nails very carefully.'

'All right,' said the pathologist. 'We'll go up now and give it to the boss.'

They found the superintendent waiting with an anxious look in his eye. They knew just what was worrying him. It was the loneliest part of the common and still not much after eight o'clock. But people were stirring. A small boy had appeared at the end of the path

14

and was fidgeting with ill-concealed excitement.

'What do you make of it?'

'Cause of death was one very heavy blow on the front of the head. Cracked the skull. No other marks that couldn't have been caused by tumbling down that slope. Scratches on hands and tears in clothes and that sort of thing. And I'd say she was lying as she would have lain after a fall.

'The only thing is, I can't see anything down there quite hard enough to have given her such a dunt on the head. There's the stump of an old fence post—but you'd think it would need something harder than that—more like a piece of iron or concrete. Unless she had an uncommonly thin skull. I'll know more about that when I've done the P.M.'

'How long has she been there?'

'Can't say exactly. But take it she was dead before midnight. And not more than 12 hours.'

'That fits in with the only witness we've got.'

'The man who found her?'

'Yes. He was past the same spot at about seven o'clock yesterday evening and says she wasn't there then. But likely as not he just didn't see her.'

'No, I think he's right. The ground underneath her is quite damp. Not soaked like the ground round it but quite damp. When did it start to rain last night, do you know?'

'Seven o'clock. And kept on pretty steadily all night.'

'Yes. Well, if you say she was in position by 10 or 11 that would fit in with most of the evidence you've got so far.'

It was all very well, thought the superintendent, but it didn't answer the real question.

'It's your decision, of course,' said the pathologist, 'but I think you'd be justified as a precaution in treating it as murder.'

His words seemed to release a spring.

'We'll want all the help we can get,' said the superintendent to Leavis. 'Carter here can telephone the station. And before you go, lay a couple of these hurdles across the path to seal this section. And get ropes to cordon off the rough between the path and the gully. And the photographers. Though goodness knows how they're going to operate.'

'Better bring some brush-hooks and a saw. And spades to cut steps. Send out a teletype with the description of the clothes, height, estimated age and so on.'

'Could you let him have those details again, Miss Bose? Then we'll want some men for searching. Ask the station sergeant to send anyone he's got. I'll square it with the chief. Use my car.'

The superintendent tucked the tails of his raincoat carefully under him and perched on

16

the edge of the gully. Craning his long neck he could just see one, pathetic, brown shoe, the toe turned downwards and a flash of scarlet ankle sock above it.

Above him the grey clouds were thinning away with a promise of sun after a night of rain. Behind and below him the smoky metropolis was grinding and grumbling its way back to another day of work. For the first time he could hear the birds.

Suddenly he smacked his hand down on to the wet trampled grass.

'What mugs we all are,' he said. 'Of course it's murder. Must be. No doubt about it. No doubt at all.'

* * *

A car turned slowly in from the main road and bumped along the gravel path, stopping at the hurdles. A little, thick, white-haired man hopped out and came across the grass. The superintendent scrambled to his feet. 'Hear you're on to something, Mahood.' . . . 'Yes, sir. It's a girl. Murder, I'm pretty sure.'

'You've had the pathologist report, then?'

'Not yet, sir.'

'Oh, I rather gathered the idea was she came along here in the dark and tumbled down this gully and smacked her head on a post.'

'She might have done that, sir. But equally

someone might have brought her here in a car and dumped her.'

'Yes. And you prefer the dumping idea. Why?'

'It was raining steadily all last night. If she did walk here, it meant quite a long walk, in the rain.'

'Girls do things like that, you know.'

'Yes, sir. But this was a girl who spent a lot of money on her appearance. She'd just had a five-guinea perm. And she had a perfectly good scarf with her. Which she was wearing *round her neck.*'

'Ah,' said the chief superintendent, slowly, 'yes, I think you might have something there. Are you going to be able to do this yourself?'

'I'd like to try.'

'Of course you would. I'll let you have 48 hours. Then we'll have to think again. Speed's the thing, of course. Particularly in a dumping case.

'People may have seen the car. Or seen her out with someone. They forget that sort of thing very quickly. A day and a night may make all the difference, and you want to get hold of her friends and relations before they've read all about it in the papers. But I needn't tell you that.'

'No, sir.'

Mahood liked and admired the chief superintendent who was in charge of all C.I.D. work in No. 3 district and therefore his immediate boss; but nobody likes being told how to do his own job.

'The thing will turn on whether you can get a quick identification. Let me know how I can help. And keep me in the picture.'

'I'll certainly do that, sir.'

Mahood watched the chief superintendent out of sight, and then sat down again.

Time. Of course, that was what mattered. Any rookie knew that. Time which obliterated footprints, scattered valuable evidence and drew a haze of uncertainty over the minds of even the most willing witnesses.

'Well, inspector, it was more than a week ago and a lot's happened since then. I can't really remember—'

Time.

Here was Sergeant Leavis back, with his reinforcements. Not a boy to waste time, the sergeant.

Mahood said to him: 'We'll rope off the whole of the rough between the two hurdles and the railway line. It's a big area, but I don't see how we can cut down on it. However she came, whether she walked or was brought, it's ten to one she was in a car as far as where the track joins the road. Then she either walked or was carried. Up the path and straight across. Or on a slant.

'I want the whole of this area picked over. Beat across it in line to see if there's anything obvious. Then go back across it very slowly.

And don't forget the railway embankment. She may have come from there. It's not so likely because the fence is in the way. But cover it.'

A party under a sergeant from the uniformed branch withdrew to plan the operation. They none of them looked happy. The thought of crawling over an acre of wet grass and thornbush was already beginning to work on them.

There were two more C.I.D. men there now. Mahood said to one of them: 'She mustn't be moved till the photographers have finished, but I want you to get down and have a good look at her yourself, height and weight and age and clothes and so on. Then go and check the Missing Persons Lists, here and at Central Office. I want results, and I want them quick.'

And to the other: 'If a car came up that road and stopped any length of time last night between say, eight o'clock and five o'clock this morning, I want to hear about it. There's an A.A. box at the foot of the hill where it comes up on to the common. The scout's a good man and may be able to help. Oh, and there's a transport café—'

But the C.I.D. man was gone. It is possible that he, also, had views on people who tried to do other people's jobs for them.

The superintendent found a sergeant at his elbow and grabbed at him, as at a straw.

'Take this piece of path between the

hurdles,' he said, 'and go over it for footprints. It's a lovely surface, and the council, bless them, had it nicely rolled last week.'

'There's quite a lot of footprints there already,' said the sergeant.

'Then you'll have quite a lot of work to do,' said the superintendent and caught the station inspector to arrange for the more effective cordoning of the area and relief for the searchers.

'I'm going back to Crown Road,' he said. 'I'll use the C.I.D. office there as headquarters. Direct all reports there. What have you got there? Oh, it's the sandwiches I asked for. Thanks very much. I'll take 'em with me. And who's this?'

A very large car had drawn up and was parking itself on the rough on the other side of the path. 'Looks like the D.C. Well, he's your pigeon. But whatever you do with him, keep him off the path.'

Back at the stuffy little room at Crown Road police station, time seemed to go slowly. The superintendent sat at the table, making notes on a piece of paper. He would much rather have been out of doors, doing something, but experience had taught him that there was a time for running round and a time for sitting still.

The telephone rang. Mahood picked up the receiver and said: 'Crown Road. Mahood here.' The voice at the other end said quite a lot.

'I'm not sure,' said Mahood at last. 'If I knew exactly what I wanted, I should know what I was looking for, if you see what I mean. But, within limits, what I want is a note of any offence. Particularly offences involving violence, that took place in London, last night between six and midnight. In fact, it needn't even have been a criminal job. Any sort of wild party or horseplay. *Anything* that might have led to a nice girl getting hit on the head.'

The voice at the other end said something, and Mahood said: 'I know it's a large order, but it can't be helped.'

Presently the telephone rang again. This time his pencil got busy. 'Let's have it slowly,' he said. And wrote, 'Pathologist. Further report received 15.05 hours. Death almost certainly due to external violence. Blow on the top front of the face. From above. Girl either sitting or crouching or assailant taller than she was. Smooth, heavy instrument. Left no splinters. Might be leather-covered cosh.

'All right. Anything on the clothes? Yes, let's have it. Slowly. "Forensic Science Laboratory. Preliminary report. 14.55 hours. Would appear all marks carefully removed from clothing. No name tabs, makers' tabs, laundry marks. Much of clothing new and well cared-for. Most stains match with samples soil and vegetation produced and probably caused by tumble down slope. Blue serge trousers older than rest of outfit. Microscope reveals minute splinters of wood, probably spruce, inches from bottom of right-hand pocket, on outside of right trouser-leg. Further report follows."

Mahood said, 'Thank you very much,' and rang off, as the door opened and Sergeant Leavis came in.

'I've seen the first photographs,' he said. 'I'm afraid there's nothing there we could give to the Press. Not without a good bit of cleaning up.'

'Bad as that, are they?'

'They're not gruesome. There's a big bruise on the forehead and nose. But the rain and the wind between them haven't improved her. I doubt her own mother would recognise her from the ones we've got so far.'

Both men were silent. Mahood knew the value of a quick Press release. But he also knew that a bad photograph could do more harm than good.

'Is there anything from Missing Persons, sir?'

'Not yet.'

'I'll be going back,' said Sergeant Leavis. 'I nearly forgot. Your wife sent these down.'

He laid an untidy brown paper parcel on the table. In it the superintendent found his pyjamas and washing and shaving kit.

Outside it was beginning to rain again.

Up on the common Sergeant Appleyard

said to his searchers: 'Let's add it up so far and see what it comes to. Eleven matchboxes, various. Nineteen fag-ends, 12 with lipstick, seven without. Shocking the way women are smoking these days. Three screwtops for beer bottles, one half-crown, two halfpennies and one coin, foreign, unidentified. What's that you've got there, Simcox?'

'I think it's the metal piece off a suspender belt, sarge.'

'You ought to know,' said Sergeant Appleyard. 'You're a married man. All right. There's another hour before it gets dark. Get cracking.'

In the C.I.D. office the telephone had fallen silent. Mahood looked at his watch. Five o'clock.

He knew very well that he had stumbled at the first hurdle. They had a good description of the girl. Knew her height and weight. Could guess her age. A first search of the Missing Lists had produced a number of likely candidates, but all of them had fallen through for one reason or another.

Now he didn't know where to start. It was worse than looking for a needle in a haystack. Given 100 policemen you could pull a haystack to pieces in time.

And yet. . . .

At the back of his mind something he had heard was teasing him. It was a pointer, if only he could put his hand on it. Something that would narrow the field right away. Something he could get started on. Something someone had said.

Outside the rain thickened.

Sergeant Leavis came in, the water running off his macintosh and forming puddles on the linoleum. 'Lovely weather for ducks,' he observed.

'Got it!' said the superintendent. 'Ducks. That's it. Give me that telephone.'

'Get me Central. Chief Superintendent Harris.' Sergeant Leavis said, 'You thought of something, sir?'

'It wasn't me, it was you,' said Superintendent Mahood. 'When you said, "Weather for ducks." Ducks, rivers; rivers, boats. Get it?'

'Sorry, sir. Not a glimmer.'

'You remember what the pathologist said when he first saw her? "Sporting type." He was thinking of the trousers. Girls wear trousers everywhere nowadays, of course. But the original idea was exercise. Open-air exercise. Right?'

'Yes, but—'

'This laboratory report I've just had says they found a number of spruce-wood splinters driven into the weave of the cloth on the outside of the right leg, between the hip and the knee and what do you get? You get a good, old-fashioned river sport. Punting.

'Hello. Yes. It's Mahood here. You were

25

good enough to say you'd help. I've got to go outside my manor a bit. Could you have a check-up made at all boat-houses that hire out punts? I've got a photograph I want shown to them.'

'We can go up as far as Staines,' said Chief Superintendent Harris. 'If it's further up river than that we'll have to rope in the county forces. They'll help, of course, but it might take a little time to get organised.'

'Try as far as Staines first,' said Mahood. 'I've got a feeling she's a London girl.'

While they were waiting the superintendent said: 'Anything from the site?'

'They've got a marvellous collection of junk. Cigarette ends and beer bottle tops and that sort of thing. Just as they were knocking off Lowcock found an earring. He swears it's a real diamond. He's got an uncle who's a pawnbroker.'

'Where did he find it?'

'On the edge of the path. About ten yards from where it joins the road.'

'I don't suppose it's anything to do with us. He'd better try it on Lost Property. Hold the fort while I go round the corner for a snack.'

Pies and tea. Any large-scale criminal investigation seemed inseparably connected with pies and tea. Hundreds of pies. Gallons of tea. All bolted in a hurry in case something was happening which ought to be attended to.

He found Leavis looking at a folder. 'It's the

footprints from the path,' he said. 'Not bad. They've isolated seventeen different prints. Nine of them look like kids'. I think the path's a short-cut to school. The other eight seem to be five male and three female. One of the male's is almost certainly the District Commander.'

The telephone rang. 'Staines Police,' said a voice. 'Is that Superintendent Mahood? Central told us to get in touch with you direct. We've got an identification for that photograph of yours. Bantam's boathouse says it's Mrs Pinner. It's no good going to the boathouse. That's shut now. But you could go to the house if it's urgent. It's a bungalow called Wee Two, Riverside Avenue—.'

'Thank you,' said Mahood.

'We'll see to it. Thanks a lot.'

He turned to Leavis. 'Mrs Pinner. Well, you can't tell. She might have left her wedding ring at home. Take a car.'

Sergeant Leavis was already out of the door.

Ten minutes later Staines came through again. 'Very sorry,' said the voice. 'False alarm. We had old Bantam in here himself just now. He says the photograph is pretty like Mrs Pinner, but a bit younger. And she's a keen punter. But it can't be her, because he saw her at lunchtime going over Staines Bridge and she waved to him.'

'Too bad,' said the superintendent. 'Never mind. Thank you for trying.'

He looked at his watch. It was too late to do anything about Leavis. If he knew the police driver, that young man was half-way to Staines already.

The woman who opened the door of Wee Two to Sergeant Leavis had her back to the light and her face was a white blur. None the less it gave the sergeant a shock. The resemblance was very marked.

'Mrs Pinner?'

'Yes. That's me. I'm afraid I haven't the pleasure——?'

'Sergeant Leavis, Metropolitan Police.'

'Oh yes. Would you like to come in?'

There was surprise there, but no alarm.

'If you wouldn't mind,' he said. 'It's just a routine check we're making. We wondered if you might be able to help us identify a photograph?'

'I'm not much good—' Her voice failed. She made a noise which sounded like 'Di' and slumped on the floor.

Sergeant Leavis caught her as she fell and swung her on to the sofa.

A key sounded in the lock and a puffy man in glasses looked round the door and said: 'Really, what is happening? Jean! Who are you?'

It took a little time to sort out, but a quarter of an hour later they were all drinking cups of strong tea, and Mrs Pinner, her face still white, was talking.

28

'It's Di,' she said. 'Diana. My sister. She's a bit younger than I am, but they say we're very much like each other.'

'There, there, chick,' said Mr Pinner. 'Don't work yourself up.'

'Just the two of you? Parents?'

'Mum and dad are both dead. Di lived with us. You see, I promised mother—'

'There, there,' said Mr Pinner. He decided that it was time that he took charge.

'You'll understand,' he said, 'that Miss Devon—my wife's sister—was 24. She had a room here. She didn't always sleep in it. She'd got lots of girl friends in town. Sometimes she'd be away three or four nights running.'

'I see. So when she didn't come home last night—'

'We never gave it a thought. As a matter of fact she hadn't been here since Sunday night.'

'Always a tomboy,' said Mrs Pinner. 'Have some more tea.'

By midnight Sergeant Leavis was back at Helenwood, with his gleanings.

'That's about the ticket,' he concluded. 'A real modern girl. Go anywhere, do anything. Boating. Riding. Ski-ing—when she could afford it. And when she couldn't, she was quite happy to bump round on the back of a friend's motor-bike or dance the soles off her shoes at the local palais.'

'Had she got a job?'

'She'd had dozens of jobs. Work hard at

29

anything until she'd earned enough money to have a good time. Then take a month off and spend it all.'

'What's she been working at lately?'

'Lately she's been on a spree. During the last three weeks she's only spent week-ends and a few odd nights at her sister's. She wasn't a girl to talk much, but there was something about horseriding. She took her riding kit up to town with her. And something about conjuring.'

'Sounds like a new boy friend.'

'I thought so, sir. And she's got a steady, too.'

'Has she now? Familiar sort of pattern. Any line on him?'

'His name's Angus Mickle. He works for Bettabix—the breakfast food people—and he's been in the Midlands on an assignment for nearly a month.'

'I think you'd better see him as soon as possible.'

'I thought so too, sir. I've got the car standing by.'

'Take a new driver. You could be there by first light. Telephone me after breakfast.'

After Leavis had gone the superintendent wrote on the pad in front of him: 'Missing three weeks?' He then drank a cup of cold tea and tried to consider the new angles sensibly.

What might a spirited girl with money in her pocket and time to spare get up to? And, more important, how could he find out about it in the limited time at his disposal?

He could start with her last employer. And her acquaintances. Make a note to tackle the sister again in the morning. And if that didn't lead anywhere, her sister could probably lay her hands on a decent photograph, which they could get into the midday editions of the evening papers. That ought to start something.

Dawn found him studying the crime reports. The Metropolis had been comparatively quiet on the previous night. One smash and grab, half a dozen loitering with intent, one gentleman who had lost his car in Mayfair, another who had lost his wallet in Soho. The usual crop of drunk and disorderlies. Nothing specifically involving violence to a nice girl of 24 in blue serge trousers.

As he was finishing an early and scrappy breakfast, Sergeant Leavis came through on the telephone. He sounded tired.

'I'm afraid Angus is out,' he said. 'I'll give you the details when I get back. But unless he took wings and flew he can't have been anywhere near Helenwood Common at any of the times that matter.'

'All right. Anything useful about the girl?'

'One thing. She stopped answering his letters after he'd been away about a week. He said he guessed she'd picked up with someone else. In fact, he said much what her sister did.

She was a wild kid, but without any vice. She'd pick up with anyone who was amusing. Then drop him.'

'Very helpful,' said the superintendent, gloomily.

Underneath 'Missing, three weeks?' he wrote. 'Would pick up anyone amusing.'

At nine o'clock the pathologist reappeared, and there was a look in his eye which meant news. 'It's just possible I've got something for you,' he said.

'I hope it's good,' said the superintendent.

'That's for you to judge. Tell me, what would you like to know most about this girl?'

'Who she spent the last fortnight with,' said Mahood, promptly.

'Nothing easier,' said the pathologist with a broad grin. 'Any time you want to know a little thing like that come straight to your medical man. I'll tell you what I've just noticed. She has long, well-formed hands, with thin, slightly tapering fingers. And the second and third fingers of her right hand are exactly equal in length.'

'Are they now?' said the superintendent slowly. 'Yes. Well, it's an idea, isn't it?'

'It's not a thing you'll see in one person in a hundred thousand,' said the pathologist. 'But those hands are pickpocket hands.'

'Scissor-fingers,' agreed the superintendent. 'If your second and third fingers are the same length you can use 'em as tongs, without having to bend the middle finger. I wonder. It's certainly worth trying.'

'Do you imagine she *was* a professional pickpocket?'

The superintendent thought for a moment. 'No,' he said. 'I don't think that fits in with what we know. But she might have been taken up by a plausible character who had some idea of training her. Pickpockets' stooges are usually girls. Particularly the high-class operators who like to get their victims either tight or thoroughly compromised before they go through them. I think this is where we ask Criminal Records to help.'

He lifted the receiver and spoke to the C.R.O., who said: 'Pickpockets, eh? We've got bags of those. London area. Smooth types with a bit of sex appeal. All right. See what we can do.'

As he put down the receiver the door opened and the white-haired chief superintendent bounced in.

'Morning, Mahood,' he said. 'Hullo, doctor. Got that thing broken yet?'

'We've got a certain way, sir. We know who the girl is. Miss Diana Devon. Respectable, middle-class background, though a bit of a wild performer herself. She lived at Staines, when she was at home. And I should think there's no doubt she was knocked on the head, somewhere in the Central London area,

33

packed into a car, and tumbled down that slope on Helenwood Common in an effort to make it look like an accident.'

'Murderer's a cool hand. Do you know who it was?'

The superintendent restrained the impulse to say 'If I knew that I wouldn't be sitting here,' and said instead, 'We've got an idea that she may have been got hold of, in the last fortnight, by a professional pickpocket who had ideas of using her as his stooge.

'The pattern of the thing would be that he jollied her along to start with—innocent conjuring tricks, and that sort of thing—but showed his hand too soon. She turns him down flat. Says she is going straight to the police. He panics, and hits her—too hard.'

'Any positive evidence of all this?'

Mahood explained about the fingers. The chief superintendent said: 'Sounds a bit thin to me.'

The chief superintendent suddenly realised that he was being tactless.

'I think you've done very well,' he said. 'You wanted a quick identification, and you got it. However, I've got to be realistic about the next step.

'And you know as well as I do, that sort of evidence disappears as quickly as mist in the morning. If we don't fix it now, we'll probably never get it. That means that we ought to get Central working on it as soon as possible.'

34

'You originally gave me forty-eight hours,' said Mahood. 'I've had just over twenty-four. Will you stick to that?'

'All right. Till ten o'clock tomorrow morning.' He stopped at the door and added with a grin: 'And don't read that as a vote of no-confidence. I think you've done very well.'

The pathologist departed and Sergeant Leavis looked in to say: 'Guess what. You remember that earring?'

'The one Lowcock found near the end of the path?'

'Yes. Well, it was the real thing. A local jeweller says it's a yellow diamond. Step-cut baguette, platinum filigree mounting, worth at least two hundred quid on its own. More as one of a pair.'

'Bit of luck for Lowcock,' said the superintendent. 'He'd better search the lost property files. I don't suppose it's anything to do with this job.'

The next call was from the Criminal Records Office.

'Here's a preliminary list of known pickpockets,' said the voice.

Mahood scribbled hard, with a lengthening face.

'Can't you cut it down any more than that?' he said. 'That's—wait while I count 'em—15 possibilities.'

'We've cut 'em down already. I gather you don't want the old lags and street-corner types. These are the smooth boys. West End operators.'

'The sort who might impose on a simple girl.'

'They'd impose on your Aunt Fanny if they thought there was a percentage in it. If you could let us have any other information— habits, clothes, age, hobbies, anything like that—we might shorten the list for you.'

'I see,' said Mahood. 'I can't do that at the moment because it's only guesswork that he exists at all. But I'll let you have anything we get.'

All the dead girl's personal belongings had been impounded and brought by car to Crown Road police station. Clothes, old and new: three bulging cardboard boxes of personal papers, two photograph albums, and miscellaneous items ranging from theatre programmes to a booklet on judo.

'The trouble is,' said Sergeant Leavis, 'that it's all such old stuff. There isn't a theatre programme or ticket stub less than three months old. And the letters are the same.'

'Have you been through the clothes?'

'Yes, sir. I think the trouble is that these are clothes she hasn't worn for some time. Then there were the ones she was in. Nothing in those.

'I should imagine that the people who knocked her on the head went through her pockets.'

36

'Yes. And any spare clothes she'd been wearing lately would be wherever it is she's been staying for the last few nights. Which we haven't found yet. We're working through her known friends now. Have there been any reactions from that photograph? I saw it in the midday *Standard*.'

'The usual crop. Most of them obviously liars or loonies. Two of them sounded possible. There was, believe it or not, an Aubrey Fetheringham-Basset who says he was at a cocktail party at a house in Paulton Square—I gather it was one of those enormous Chelsea cocktail parties where everyone thinks everyone has been brought by someone else.

'He says he noticed the girl, not because she was wearing trousers—half the guests were wearing trousers—but failed because the girl was too much taken up with a man, fortyish, black haired, a nasty type, our Aubrey says—but that may simply have been jealousy—who practically kidnapped the girl in his big green saloon car; and that was that.'

'Nothing much to go on.'

'No. The other was Mr Bonsor. A nice little old man. A groom at Cuthbert's Livery Stable in Knightsbridge. He says she's ridden there every weekday morning for the last two weeks. But she came alone, and left alone. And didn't talk to him. So that's that.'

The telephone rang again. Sergeant Leavis,

37

who was nearest, answered it. 'It's Mrs Pinner,' said a voice. 'Could I speak to someone—oh, it's you, is it, sergeant?'

'That's right, ma'am. What can I do for you?'

'I'd like them back if you've finished with them.'

'You'd like—?'

'I'd like the trousers back.'

The superintendent, who was listening on an extension, said: 'Tell her she can't have 'em. Important evidence.'

'But,' said the telephone, plaintively, 'how *can* they be evidence? They weren't even Di's trousers. They were mine. I lent them to her when she fell into the river that weekend and got her own wet through. Hers are in the drying-cupboard—'

'Are they, though?' said Sergeant Leavis. He looked at the superintendent, who nodded. 'Then if you don't mind, I'll come right out and collect them.'

'Couldn't it wait until tomorrow?' said Mrs Pinner. 'I'm just going to bed.'

'Stay up till I come,' said Sergeant Leavis. 'I shan't be long.'

It took him 50 minutes to get out to Staines, which was fast going. But he got back even faster. The superintendent saw from the look in his eyes that a long shot had come off.

It was a bill from a well-known West End multiple store for a pair of doe-skin gloves. It was stained with river water, and crumpled, but quite legible.

'Look at the date, sir,' said Sergeant Leavis. 'Only 10 days ago. And there's something on the back.'

The writing had been done in capital letters, with an indelible pencil. On top was 'YET COO.' And under that 'BART BOW DAN.'

'Well,' said the superintendent. 'That could be a break. It tells us how she spent part of her evenings, anyway, doesn't it? We'll need two cars. And I think I'll come with you myself. Do you know. I've a feeling this thing may be coming out?'

As the two police cars race south, towards the centre of London, Sergeant Leavis said to Superintendent Mahood, unusual deference in his voice: 'I wonder, sir, if you could—er—outline to us what we're going to do.'

'You mean you don't understand that paper you found in her pocket?'

'I'm afraid not, sir. I knew it might be important, because it was recent. That's all.'

'If a girl scribbles down "Yet Coo" and "Bart Bow Dan" on the back of a bit of paper, it means that someone has been introducing her to the pleasures of Chinese food. If she was an old hand, she wouldn't trouble to write those two down, she'd be bound to know them. "Yet Coo" is noodle soup and "Bart Bow Dan's" a sort of ham omelette.'

'I see, sir. And you think this chap she

picked up with took her out to Chink eating places. It certainly fits. If she was a pickpocket and planned to use her as an accomplice he certainly wouldn't want to be seen with her under the bright lights.'

At West End Central Police Station they found Inspector Pickup, who, as a sergeant, had worked under Mahood at Scotland Yard.

He pulled down a wall map. 'Unless you're going for a real Chinese eater—something down in the docks, I mean—' Mahood shook his head—'then we've only got three main groups to cover. There are a few in Bloomsbury, another lot in the Charing Cross Road, and, of course, there's Soho.

'If you split into three parties I'll lend you one of my men to go with each party and you should get round the lot before the night's out.'

Detective Constable Byloe, who accompanied the superintendent's party, was a brisk young man. He seemed to be on Christian name terms with every restaurateur between Wardour Street and Soho Square. At three o'clock in the morning they struck oil. Ah Foong's International and Celestial Restaurant was a tiny, frosted-glass-fronted rabbit hutch in Scrope Street. One square room opening directly on to the street. Byloe leaned against the bell until the door was opened.

A very wide-awake old gentleman said:

'Come in. Mr Byloe. Come in, gentlemen. Nothing wrong, I hope.' He turned on another light and showed them into the deserted dining-room. There was the noise of subdued activity somewhere in the back.

Ah Foong grinned and said: 'My sister's birthday.'

'Today or yesterday?' said Byloe. 'Never mind. The superintendent here wants to ask you some questions.'

Mahood produced a well-worn photograph and said: 'I wondered if—'

'That girl,' said Ah Foong. 'I know her well. She comes here often. With a man.'

'How long have they been coming here?'

'The man comes here, oh, many years. The girl, just two, three weeks.'

Mahood picked up the printed menu. Sure enough. 'Yet Coo' and 'Bart Bow Dan' were actually on the table d'hôte.

'Would you recognize this man?'

'You give me photograph. I recognize him quick.'

'That's fine,' said Mahood. 'I think we'll go back to the station now.'

Though his body was desperately weary, a small section of his brain still seemed to be functioning. From West End Central Station he put through a call to the night duty officer at Scotland Yard.

He said, 'Criminal Records made a short list for me yesterday. Fifteen male pickpockets,

41

operating in London. I'd very much like photographs of all of them.

'I've had a list of crime reports from you. I'm speaking from memory, but I think one was a complaint of a wallet, lost at a restaurant in the Soho area. Could you look that one up for me and telephone anything you get.'

An impromptu breakfast, produced by Sergeant Butt, restored Mahood's vitality. He recognized the constable who brought in the enamel jug of dark brown steaming tea.

'You're Lowcock, aren't you?' he said. 'You found the earring.'

'That's right, sir. All the smart Alecs said it was a Woolworth's Special, but I knew better. Real diamond and platinum. Mrs Rosegarten reported it. She's coming here to get it.'

'When was it reported lost?'

'It's been on the list about three weeks, sir.'

The flicker of interest in Mahood's mind died, stillborn. The earring had been picked up on the edge of the path, only a few yards in from the road, at exactly the spot where a car might have stopped. But if it had been lost three weeks ago, it had nothing to do with the murder.

In the next hour the news was all good.

First came Inspector Pickup. 'Ah Foong has come through,' he said. 'He's identified a photograph of the man who was with the girl. He's Harry Carfax, alias Harry Carfew, alias lots of other things. A very high-class picker, of upper-class pockets.

'You know the lark. He shares a flat in Chelsea with a woman who passes as his sister for business reasons. Actually, so far as the records go, she's his one and only lawful wedded wife. And—here's the point—she used to be his stooge. Getting a bit too slow and too fat now. Does it add up?'

'Thank you,' said Mahood. 'I think it's adding up.'

Next came Sergeant Dent with a report on the footprints from the path beside the body. 'We've identified a lot of them,' he said. 'All of the children; they're just local kids. And four of the men and two of the women. That leaves one male and one female unaccounted for.'

Next came Detective Constable Flagg. The painstaking method of door-to-door inquiry had at last produced the small piece of the jigsaw.

'Miss Deans, sir. Lives in one of the council houses on South Wood Drive. Says she didn't like to come forward, bless her, because she'd been out with a boy friend and her mother didn't approve of him.

'However, the two of them—I've seen the boy, too—quite a good witness—works in a garage—were in the shelter, just off the road, on top of the common, and they saw a car. They noticed it because it was parked on the rough, clear of the road, with all lights out.

The boy said he guessed there was another couple courting. A big green car.'

'What time was this?'

'Near one o'clock in the morning.'

'Did he get the number of the car? Or the make?'

'I'm afraid not, sir. They didn't go too close, for fear of being thought nosey-parkers.'

'Of course. That's very good work, Flagg.'

'If Carfax has got a big green car?' said Sergeant Leavis, 'I'd say we were home.'

He looked up when the superintendent didn't answer and added: 'Don't you think so, sir?'

'No,' said Mahood. 'I don't. We may get there eventually, but we're not there yet. It's only a story so far. A story in two parts. Down in the West End there's Harry Carfax. Gentleman pickpocket with six aliases, a wife, and (maybe) a green car. Up on Helenwood Common there's a nice girl, dead. She was dumped (maybe) from a green car.

'What we need now is one single, indisputable water-tight, lawyer-proof piece of evidence to join the two. And we've got—' he looked at the clock—'precious little time to find it.'

They both saw the taxi arrive. They both saw the middle-aged lady in the mink top coat get out into the rain, erect a long-handled scarlet umbrella, and stump across to the police station entrance.

44

The taxi waited.

'Who's that?' said Sergeant Leavis.

'I'd guess that it's Mrs Rosegarten. Come to claim one diamond earring.'

'Bit old, but plenty of figure,' said Sergeant Leavis. 'Let's go and have a look at her.'

In the charge room Mrs Rosegarten, advancing behind a protective screen of Nuit d'Amour, stepped up to Sergeant Butt's desk, fumbled in a snake-skin handbag, and placed down on the desk something that sparkled coldly under the electric light.

'I've come for its twin,' she said. 'I'm told you've got it.'

'We have had an earring handed in,' admitted Sergeant Butt, with professional caution. 'Perhaps you could tell us where you lost yours.'

''Ow should I know where I lost it? In the morning I put it on. In the evening, when I come to take it off, it's gone. We'd been out in the car with my husband—round London—all over the place. What's it matter, now you've found it?'

Sergeant Butt unlocked a safe behind his desk, produced a second earring and laid it beside the first. They were indeed a perfect match.

'If you'll just sign this form,' he said.

Five minutes later it was all over. Mrs Rosegarten took delivery of her earring, paid the reward without demur, in new pound notes, and stumped out.

It was as the door closed behind her that Superintendent Mahood appeared to go mad. He jumped at Sergeant Butt who was moving to shut the door, and hit him in the chest so hard that he nearly knocked him down. Then he jumped to the window and peered through it. The taxi was disappearing into the drizzle.

'Get a move on, man,' he shouted to the startled Leavis. 'There's our first real bit of evidence. And it'll be gone in two minutes.'

Sergeant Leavis gaped at the superintendent. 'Get a camera. And someone who can use it. Hurry.' Sergeant Leavis hurried. Ten seconds later he was back with a big, black, tripod camera. 'I know how to use it,' he said breathlessly. 'But what—'

'That damp footprint on the linoleum, by the door. If you get the camera right down— you, sergeant, shine that desk lamp on it, sideways. If we get an oblique light across it we may catch it. Right. And again. As many shots as you can get.'

'You take the measurements,' the superintendent said to Butt. 'I'll do the drawing.'

The white-haired chief superintendent, who came in at that moment, stared in surprise at the three men on their knees.

'Lost something?' he said.

'No, sir.' Superintendent Mahood straightened up. 'I think we've found something. If you'd care to come with me to the C.I.D. room we'll be able to see if my hunch is right.'

A few minutes later the three of them were looking through a folder. From it the superintendent drew out a full-scale facsimile drawing of a footprint.

'I think you're right,' said the chief superintendent. 'In fact, I'm sure you are. They're both the same size, both with rubber-tipped heels and non-skid rubber soles with diagonal ribbing, very much worn down on the left side.'

'And you see that line, sir. Right across the ribbing. The photographs we took ought to catch that. It's a cut. Someone's been cleaning the soles with a knife and it's slipped.'

'I'd like to get hold of the original shoe to be sure.'

'We can get it, sir. If you'll let us.'

The chief superintendent cocked an eye at Mahood.

'You're ready to charge someone?'

'Two people, sir.'

'One, I take it, would be the lady who departed in a taxi as I arrived. And who presumably, left this footprint behind her. Who is she, by the way?'

'She called herself Mrs Rosegarten, but I have every reason to suspect that she's Mrs Carfax or Carfew. She poses as the "sister", and is in fact the wife, of Harry Carfax, a convicted larcenist. His special line is picking high-class pockets.'

'Have you got time to tell me the story?'

'Certainly, sir. I'd like to try it on someone to see how good it sounds.'

'Treat me as the jury.'

'Right, sir.' The telephone interrupted him. He snatched up the receiver. Said, 'Yes.' And a bit later, 'Oh, did he?' and a bit later, still, 'Had he really? That's good. Thanks.'

The chief superintendent had been listening in on the extension. He said, 'From the expression on your face I gather that it's good news to you that Harry Carfax keeps a small livery stable in Knightsbridge, and runs a large, green saloon car. I don't pretend to understand it myself, but no doubt you will be able to enlighten me.'

'I'll try, sir. The story starts with Diana Devon, a nice girl, but a bit wild. Her parents are dead, and she lived with her sister at Staines. When I say "lived" I mean she had a room there, and used it when it suited her. Other nights she'd spend in town—with girl friends. She liked life. And she met Harry Carfax. At a big cocktail party in Chelsea. He was a pickpocket who worked with a girl stooge. His wife had stooged for him for years. But she was past it. He wanted a substitute.'

'I don't suppose his wife was keen on the idea.'

'I don't think she was consulted, sir. Anyway, as soon as he saw Diana, he thought, this is it. Right type, if he could induce her to play. And, by a fluke, she herself had "pickpocket hands." Long fingers, the second and middle one about the same length.

'So he fastened on to her. Jollied her along. Gave her free riding at his livery stable. Took her out to back-street restaurants. And I should think, posed as an amateur conjuror. Diana mentioned conjuring to her sister when she was home one week-end.

'Harry could take her back to his flat—his "sister" acting as a chaperon. And I've no doubt he gave her a very good time and soon had her eating out of his hand.'

'Yes,' said the chief superintendent. 'Then your idea would be that he tried to rush her on a bit quick.'

'I'd go further than that,' said Mahood. 'I think I know just when and where it happened. He used to take her a lot to Ah Foong's Restaurant in Scrope Street.

'And one evening, I suggest, he pointed to the next table and said: "See old Bill there. He hasn't recognized me yet. You remember that pocket-picking trick I showed you. Wouldn't it be fun to see if we can get his wallet? We'll both go out when he does—I'll jostle him in the doorway, and when he turns round you see if you're quick enough to lift it." Which they do. Successfully.

49

'Back at the flat Diana says, "Well, now let's ring up Bill and have our laugh." Whereupon Harry breaks it to her that he doesn't know Bill from Adam. And there's fifty pounds in notes in the wallet.

'Being a perfectly honest girl, and not liking the look in his eyes, she jumps for the telephone with the idea of dialing 999 and he panics and coshes her, a lot too hard. His wife comes back five minutes later, and finds him with a dead body on his hands.

'Later that night, when things are quiet, they take the body down to the car—tricky bit, that. But they may have a private back entrance to the mews where the car is. Then out to Helenwood Common, and dump her.'

'Yes, but look here,' said the chief superintendent, 'you've got on to this woman, because she comes to claim a diamond earring she's lost, and which has been found 10 yards from where the body was dumped.'

'Right.'

'But she reported the loss *three weeks ago.* Do you mean to tell me that, by coincidence, she went up to the same spot three weeks before she helped dump the body there?'

'It worried me, too,' said Mahood with a smile. 'Until I saw what must have happened. She told us she lost the earring when she was out in the car. Well, that was true.

'It came off and fell somewhere down under the footrest or floor carpet, beside the rear

50

door. And lay there. Until this particular night, when they were dragging the girl out of the car, in the pitch dark and rain, and dragged the earring out with her.'

'Could be,' said the chief superintendent. 'Now, what have we got in the way of actual evidence?'

'Ah Foong will say that Carfax has been seen about with the girl for the last three weeks. The Carfaxes have got a big green car, which was on Helenwood Common, at the right time and in the right place. And certainly one of them—probably both—left a footprint on the path beside the spot where the body was found. I'm for charging them and asking them to explain their movements that night. Then they'll tell a pack of lies. And that'll give us some more to go on.'

The chief superintendent thought about it. Then suddenly he grinned.

'All right,' he said. 'I'm sure you're right. I believe it. You've done very well. Taken a lot of awkward hurdles. There's one question left.'

'And what's that?' asked Mahood. But he knew. It was always the final inescapable, all-important question.

'Will the jury believe it?'

THE RULES OF THE GAME

Dorothy Mayotte Rigby lay in bed, listening to the bombs. By the spring of 1941, the Germans had abandoned that indiscriminate scattering of high explosives over London, christened the Blitz. Now their bombing was more selective. Tonight it was the docks that were catching it.

If anything did happen to her, in her flat at the top of the house, it would happen with merciful speed. An old friend of hers had been trapped in a ground floor flat in Paddington and had been burned to death before the rescue squads could reach her. For the last half hour, as they cut their way through to her, they had heard her screaming.

The thud of an explosion, a little closer.

She was also an old-fashioned patriot. When the unemphatic Midland-businessman's voice of Neville Chamberlain had told them that they were at war with Germany, her wish had been, simply, to help her country to the fullest extent of her ability. So many people had felt the same that it had not been easy. In the end she had secured two jobs. By day she was one of a team of secretaries who worked for Hugh Dalton in the Ministry of Economic Warfare; unaware, as were most people, that he was also the founder and head of Special Operations

Executive.

At the end of a long day's work in the office she went to help in an inter-services canteen in Westminster. This kept her busy until midnight. By the time she got home she was usually so tired that sleep came easily.

On this occasion she had something else to take her mind off the bombs. The message had come from none other than Portland, now one of Dalton's P.A.'s. If she was interested in a special and rather important job, would she present herself, at noon on the following day, at the Northumberland Hotel?

Special and important. Certainly she would do so. She went to sleep happily.

When she arrived, the custodian checked her name on a list and she followed a Boy Scout messenger up two flights of stairs. The room she was shown into might have been, once, a second-class bedroom. The peace-time furnishings had been removed and replaced by a trestle table and three hard chairs.

The man who got up as she came in was a surprising contrast to the room. His beautifully cut pin-striped suit, cream shirt with thick gold cuff-links, his Rifle Brigade tie and the glimpse of a thin platinum watch chain across his double-breasted waistcoat would all have been very much at home in the ante-room of the Savoy Grill or propping up the Berkeley Bar. It was Denham.

'Miss Rigby?' The voice matched the clothes. 'Rupert Denham. Simla—Scotland. And now Whitehall. Glad you decided to come.'

'I could scarcely refuse,' she said, 'when the job was described as special and important.'

'Yes. Both those things, certainly. Dangerous, too. I should make it clear that you have every right to say "No".'

'Perhaps I had better hear about it first.'

'Of course. Not reasonable to blame a horse for refusing a jump before you have even led him up to it.'

In years to come she sometimes looked back on this as the beginning of a long association. They were weighing each other up.

'I shall have to start by explaining to you something of what is going on in France. For reasons that you will appreciate, I will keep much of this information general, not specific.'

'Of course.'

'The organisation which I represent has succeeded, in the months since France fell, in establishing circuits of men and women who are helpful to our cause. Twelve of them operate in the Unoccupied Zone, where life is somewhat easier. Five in the Occupied Zone. And of these, four are heading for disaster.'

Saying this he had slid into French, smooth, unaccented, adorned with the occasional piece of slang. His mind seemed to run on horses. When speaking of impending disaster he had called it 'falling at the fences'.

'The exception is the Oberon circuit. It operates in both zones. In the Nevers-Dijon area just north of the dividing line and around Vichy to the south of it. As to why it has proved more successful than the others, I must be frank with you: the other circuits are amateurs, despatched from here, brave and well-intentioned. All the members of the Oberon circuit are professionals nominated by de Gaulle himself, before he came to this country, from the lower ranks of the French Army intelligence service and the police. Two of them certainly have criminal records. They owe their prime allegiance to the General, but they are administered by us and they report to us. The flow of Intelligence material they have given us, to say nothing of their active help to escaping prisoners, has been quite invaluable. To lose them would be a major set-back.'

'And is there some danger,' said Rigby, also in French, 'that this circuit may fail?'

Since he seemed fond of race-course language she used the word *'se dégonfler'*, a piece of argot applied to a horse which refuses a jump. Denham listened carefully while she was speaking. Like an oral examiner, she thought. She was not worried. His French was smooth but hers, she was confident, was as good. And possibly more up-to-date.

'Until recently,' said Denham, reverting to English, 'one would have said that the Oberon circuit was operating in complete safety and would continue to do so. Our confidence stemmed from the method in which it had been set up. The other four groups I mentioned were composed of friends, known to each other and operating as a team. In sending them into the field we had under-estimated the techniques and the brutality of the Gestapo. First they picked up one member of the group and got to work on him. Sooner or later, according to his power of resistance, they extracted the names and particulars of all the others. These could then be rounded up at leisure. That is precisely what has happened to two of our circuits and is a constant threat to the other two. You follow me?'

Rigby nodded. She was finding speech difficult as she faced up to the expression 'got to work on'. If Denham noticed this he refrained from comment.

'The Oberon circuit on the other hand is formed on what they call the *"méthode d'échelle"*—the ladder system. Each member of it knows only one other, his "contact". If any member of the circuit were taken, his "contact" would be removed, if possible, to a place of safety—probably to Switzerland, thus preventing the infection from spreading. Only the head of the group would know everyone, but in this case he was above suspicion: a retired state prosecutor, a cosmopolitan with as many friends in Germany as in France, a landowner in the Digoin area, conveniently situated almost on the dividing line between the occupied and unoccupied zones—Henri d'Espagne.'

'Of the Château de Belle Espérance?'

'Correct. And I fancy you knew his daughter, Claudette.'

'Very well indeed. She was a great friend at school and afterwards I stayed with the family in France. Are you telling me that she is involved in this?'

'She is indeed involved. When d'Espagne, who died last month of his third and most massive heart attack, was setting up the circuit for de Gaulle he used her as a messenger and intermediary. His own health was already making travelling difficult. She was his eyes and his voice. She went everywhere and knew everyone. When we understood this, we had one paramount objective: *to remove Claudette from France.*'

'And she has refused to leave?'

'It is difficult to argue and to persuade when one's only contact is by coded message, passed through different hands. We have concluded that the only method likely to succeed is by personal contact.'

'So when do I start?'

The directness of this took even so imperturbable a character as Rupert Denham by surprise. After a long moment he said, 'It was certainly our intention to offer you this assignment. You seem to be uniquely fitted for it. But normally we should have advised you to sleep on it.'

She said with a smile, 'A night's sleep is unlikely to change my mind. And a well-placed bomb might remove your candidate.'

'True.'

'I imagine that speed is important.'

'It is vital. Circumstances might direct the attention of the Gestapo to Claudette at any moment.'

'Then you may take it that I am ready to go immediately.'

'I wish that were true. Unfortunately it is not. It will take a fortnight, probably more, to give you the minimum training. And that will mean compressing into two weeks a course which normally takes two months. However, there are a number of items which can be dispensed with in your case.' He ticked them off on his fingers. 'Parachute training. Unnecessary. Entry by parachute is a one-way operation. In your case we aim to get you out with Claudette, so a different method will be chosen. Wireless and code drill. Unnecessary. General commando and fitness training. I have young Portland's word that you played five games of squash with him recently, and left him on his knees.'

'Leslie's fat and chair-borne. But yes, I am reasonably fit.'

'Then that leaves three items. First, tactical training. What to expect when travelling in France. What help to look for, what action to take in emergencies. Second, your own cover story. You are Madeleine Lamotte, travelling throughout the Haute Loire district, getting orders for your uncle's glassware and china business. Finally, and most important, you must be taught how to kill. Both with knife and gun and with less conventional weapons. Above all, how to kill silently.'

'That seems a moderately full fortnight's work,' agreed Rigby.

*   *   *

Exactly three weeks later she was occupying the corner seat of an 'omnibus' carriage in a train which, if it ran to time, would reach Le Donjon in half an hour.

Of those three weeks the first two had been as hard as she had expected them to be. It had not been so much the physical training which, in her case, had mostly been swimming length after length in the Olympic Baths at Hammersmith. Excellent exercise for all her muscles. And she had enjoyed the pistol practice and the unarmed combat on which her instructor, a male chauvinist, had reported 'Remarkable progress—for a woman'. It was the classroom work which had tired her. The advice and instruction which had to be memorised, the ceaseless repetition of names and places.

She wondered whether her life, up to that point, might have produced a hard body and a soft mind. A disquieting thought, if true.

At the end of the second week a Sunderland flying-boat had taken her to Gibraltar. After a wait of forty-eight hours on the Rock she had boarded a submarine with an amazingly youthful skipper which had surfaced, after an unexciting interval, off a beach some way east of Toulon. She had been ferried ashore by a French sailor who had removed his sailor's cap as soon as he landed, put on a chauffeur's cap and led her to an aged green Citroen which was parked in the sandhills. In this he had driven her to a villa on the outskirts of Toulon where he had handed her over to a comfortable, middle-aged lady whom he addressed as 'Duchesse'. This, she guessed, was a cover name, not a title.

She was, by now, sufficiently well instructed in the etiquette of clandestine travel not to enquire her hostess's real name, but there was one matter which she had to pursue. She said, when they were sitting together in the *art nouveau* lounge that evening, 'I was told that, once I was in France, all my instructions would come from a certain Michel. Ought I to make contact with him?'

'Ah, Michel!' Duchesse said. 'What a man!'

Feeling, perhaps, that this had not fully dealt with her point she added, 'It is not easy for him to communicate, as I am sure you will understand. However, I heard from him, through a friend, this morning. You will be going from here by train to Le Donjon, but not today. Today a special control has been imposed by the police. On the orders of the Germans, it is said.'

'Do you know why?'

'Maybe they are looking for someone. Who knows? Meanwhile, make yourself comfortable. Tomorrow I hope you will be able to go forward.'

It occurred to Rigby that, even if there was a control on the train, her papers being in perfect order and her cover watertight, it need not have stopped her. She was beginning to feel that she was part of a machine which was moving at its own pace, not at hers, and she was not entirely comfortable about this.

By the following morning it seemed that the control had been relaxed. Before she left the villa Duchesse gave her a handsome cockade in the form of a spray of fern leaves. 'Wear it when you arrive,' she said. 'It will bring you good fortune.' Rigby gathered that it was some form of recognition signal. The green Citroen appeared with the same driver and she was deposited in the forecourt of Toulon station where she acquired, without difficulty, a ticket for Le Donjon and a seat on the Lyon express. At Lyon she changed on to a slower train which dawdled across country to Vichy where she changed for a second time, on to a train composed entirely of half-empty omnibus-class carriages. The slow rhythm of the train matched her thoughts.

Her main preoccupation was the invisible Michel. Perhaps he would meet her at Le Donjon. She had pinned the cockade ostentatiously on to the lapel of her smart jacket. But when she stepped down from the carriage it attracted the attention only of a schoolboy, who sidled up and said, 'M'selle Lamotte?' and, when she nodded, 'Can you ride a bicycle, *ma mere*?'

She said, 'I was riding a bicycle before you were out of your nappies'.

The boy grinned and led the way out through a door labelled 'Personnel de CNF'. Here two ancient bicycles were propped against the wall. The boy strapped the capacious waterproof shoulder bag which held all her possessions on to the back of his own machine and pedalled off through the maze of back streets behind the station.

Her destination this time was a top-storey flat in a new looking block. The door was opened by a brown-faced middle-aged man with an impressive white moustache. An ex-soldier, she guessed, and was not surprised to

62

find that his cover name was 'the Colonel'. He apologised for the absence of his wife, who was out shopping, and showed her her room.

From the window Rigby could see the low ridge of hills behind which, as she knew, ran the upper waters of the Loire. She got out the Michelin map and studied it. She felt that it was high time that she took charge of her own destiny.

Later that afternoon, when his wife had still not reappeared, the Colonel suggested that they walk out to meet her. Rigby agreed willingly. She had had enough of sitting about. Also it amused her to realise that the old buck was delighted at the thought of parading with her.

The streets were full of shoppers and strollers.

'No Germans in uniform here,' said the Colonel. 'We are south of the line. Plenty of the other sort. Grey slugs.' He indicated a party of three who occupied a table in front of the principal cafe. *'Vert-de-gris,* we call them.' He inspected them with distaste.

They were a curious trio. Two of them were bulky, pale-faced, soberly dressed men who might have come from a business or civil service background.

'Gestapo, without doubt,' said the Colonel. 'I can smell them.'

Between them sat a French youth whose outfit contrasted sharply with that of his

63

companions. He was wearing a long jacket with slits in the back, tight trousers and two-tone shoes. His blond hair was a great deal longer than the Army would have approved.

'A *zazou*,' said the Colonel. 'A nancy boy. The Germans use them as spies. They should be exterminated.' He had not troubled to lower his voice. 'Ah, here is my dear wife, at last.'

The Colonel's lady was encumbered with her shopping and Rigby hastened to relieve her of some of it. The Colonel did not assist. Evidently he believed that soldiers did not carry parcels.

That evening, fortified by an excellent dinner, Rigby decided that the time had come to make her feelings clear to her host. She was grateful, she said, for the careful organisation which had brought her so far on her journey. But the time had come for her to cease being carried like a registered parcel. She must stand on her own feet.

She explained some of this to the Colonel, who listened courteously. She said, 'From the map I see that we are twenty kilometres from Digoin. From there, perhaps, another seven to my destination, the Château de Belle Espérance.'

'I regret that you should have told me that.'

'You didn't know?'

'In our trade, knowledge is only shared when it is necessary. My part is to look after you until I get further instructions.'

'From Michel?'

'From him, or through him.'

'But why must we wait? I could reach the château from here on foot and return the same night with the girl I have come to fetch.'

'You forget one thing. There is a frontier to cross. The line between the Unoccupied and the Occupied Zones. At this point it runs along the Loire. There are bridges, of course. Large ones at Digoin and Dompierre. Smaller ones in between.'

'They are guarded?'

'Some of them, some of the time. However, there are men who regularly make the trip across the line. Food is still plentiful in this zone. It is becoming much scarcer in the other.'

'Then these men are blackmarketeers. And I am to attach myself to them?'

'It would seem logical. They have the necessary knowledge and skill. I think that Michel will arrange matters in this way.'

'Michel!' said Rigby, trying to keep the impatience out of her voice. 'Who is he? Have you ever met him?'

'Never. But in the circles I move in, his suggestions are treated as orders.'

'*My* orders emphasised that speed was important. I am prepared to wait until tomorrow night, but no longer.'

The Colonel awarded her a tolerant smile.

As it fell out, her patience was not to be tried to breaking point. At dusk on the following day a vehicle drew up in the back yard of the block. It was an old army three-tonner, designed for transporting goods but adapted for carrying people by the insertion of a bench along each side under the canvas tilt at the back. The driver, a bird-like Provençal, hopped down and entered into earnest conversation with the Colonel. It was clear to Rigby that she was the subject of it.

She half hoped that she might secure the seat by the driver, but this was occupied by a fat, red-faced brute—a Belgian by his accent—who clearly had no intention of giving it up. She moved round to examine the back. There were five men already in it, three on one side and two on the other. The space between their feet was crammed with bales and bundles. While she was hesitating, a friendly hand helped her and her shoulder bag over the tailboard. She had barely time to lean out and say goodbye to the Colonel when they were off.

It was a curious journey. Avoiding the *route nationale* they stuck to the smallest of side roads. At every crossing they halted and an animated discussion took place between the driver and the Belgian. He had opened up a corner of the curtain between the front and rear of the truck, thus involving the other passengers in the debate. It seemed to Rigby that he usually had the last word.

She had memorised the map very carefully and a glimpse of the word Talent on a signboard told her that they must be intending to use the bridge at La Varenne. This would suit her well. As soon as they were across the river she could complete her journey on foot.

It was in the hamlet of St Radegonde that she changed her mind.

They had drawn up in the square opposite an *estaminet,* and this time the driver had dismounted and was talking to someone who had been standing in the doorway. The Belgian, who seemed to disapprove of this, was leaning across the driver's seat prepared to dominate the discussion. The other passengers were craning forward to see what was happening.

At this moment a van came into the square from the north. As it swung round its headlights lit up the doorway. The man who had been standing there drew back quickly, but not quickly enough.

It was the blond youth who had been sitting with the two Gestapo men in the cafe.

A tactical precept which had been drilled into Rigby said: if you are heading for disaster, do something unexpected and do it quickly.

She muttered to the friendly man on her right, 'I alight here,' lifted the canvas, slid down over the tailboard on to the cobbles and took to her heels.

Behind her a volley of voices had broken out, but she was already clear of the square and dodging round the church. She was confident she would not be followed. The truck had its own programme and would not hang about.

As soon as she was out of the village she abandoned the road and took to the fields. Thank God for S.O.E. training. No need for a compass. The pointers of the Great Bear and the bright eye of the Pole Star showed her the way. By keeping north with a little west in it she must reach the Loire downstream from Varenne.

When she slid down the bank on to the shingle Rigby saw that the river, though nothing like as formidable as in its lower reaches, was broader than she had imagined. She stripped naked, packed her clothes into the top of the shoulder bag, drew the string tightly and fastened it across her shoulders.

The water still had the chill of winter in it. She struck out, swimming a sedate breast stroke to keep her bag out of the water. Ten minutes later she was crouched on the north bank, drying herself on a scrap of towel. It was ten o'clock.

The Château de Belle Espérance, when she had stayed there in peace-time, had not been notable for early nights. In war-time it might be different. However, when she arrived, she was relieved to see lights on in many of the rooms.

It had been quite an easy approach march. She had halted once, at the sound of gun-fire away on the right, but she had met no one. A grey-haired man who answered the door peered at her and said, with a mixture of surprise and alarm, 'M'selle Rigby!'

'Indeed, Gaston. I have come to see your mistress. On business,' she added sharply when he seemed to hesitate.

'M'selle Claudette is in the small salon. But—'

'No need to announce me. I know the way.'

After a moment's hesitation the old man stepped aside and she ran up the stairs, opened the door of the smaller of the two salons and stepped in.

Claudette d'Espagne, who had been sitting at her desk, writing, swung round in her chair. She did not, as she would have done in the old days, jump up and embrace Dorothy. She seemed to have aged ten years. The eyes were narrower, the mouth was harder. It was no longer the face of a girl. It was the face of a wary and disillusioned woman.

She said, in a voice which matched her expression, 'What in the world are you doing here? How did you get here? What do you want?'

'To persuade you, I sincerely hope, to come

69

back with me to England.'

A long silence. Then, 'I see. A follow-up to two rather curious messages I received, whose object I found it difficult to understand.'

'The object was very simple. It was to save you from the attentions of the Gestapo.'

Claudette laughed. It was not a pleasant sound. She said, 'Perhaps you would be good enough, my dear Rigby, to explain why *I* should be afraid of the Gestapo. They are policemen. The only people who are afraid of policemen are criminals.'

It was clear to Rigby by now that her mission was in tatters. This new Claudette had no intention of leaving France. To discover how far the change had gone she said, with an edge in her voice, 'You realise that it was not you alone that we wished to protect? It was the members of your father's organisation.'

'As I thought. Then let me tell you that I have only recently discovered how my father was duped. The men you are speaking of are not patriots. No. Many of them are criminals. And all of them are traitors. Avowed followers of the self-styled General Charles de Gaulle.'

Rigby was aware that many Frenchmen disliked de Gaulle, but she had never heard his name pronounced with such venom. Claudette must have noted the look on her face because she said, speaking more rationally but just as bitterly, 'How can you, sitting smugly at home, have any idea of our feelings? When your army ran away at Dunkirk, it was father Pétain who came to our assistance. He is not only the lawful head of our Government, he is our hero. We do not forget the victories and sacrifices of Verdun. He is the living symbol of our last victory. It is to him that we owe our loyalty and our obedience. And I must warn you that he has decreed that anyone who assists or conceals a traitor is himself a traitor.'

'And so,' said Rigby coldly, 'you would defile your father's honour by handing over his friends to imprisonment and torture?'

'A fate which they have brought on themselves.'

'And me, too, no doubt?'

'Certainly not. I have no quarrel with you. You have been duped as my father was.'

(The gun was in its holster, under her left arm. Her duty was now quite clear.)

'Also, I promise you that I shall not say a word until you have had every chance to return to your own country.'

(But was she capable of carrying out, in cold blood, the execution of someone who had been her friend? Even if that friendship had, sadly, been lost?)

By hesitating, she had forfeited any chance she might have had. Someone had come into the room. Rigby was unsurprised to see the blond youth. He had a gun in his hand, an obscene-looking weapon, with its bulbous silencer.

He said to her, 'Turn round and face the wall'. She had no thought of refusing. Then he fired, twice. Out of the corner of her eye she saw Claudette rise on to her toes, as though she was dancing, and then crumple on to the carpet.

The boy bent forward and shot her carefully through the back of the neck. He said, 'I did not want you to see that. She was, I understand, your friend. I think it will be best if we go now? Yes?'

When Rigby tried to think about it afterwards, she was unable to recollect with any clearness the events of the next few minutes. She knew only that they left the chateau by a side door and started across the park at a brisk trot. By the time they reached the wall and the aged car which was parked outside it, the night air and the exercise had combined to restore her senses.

'If we encounter trouble,' the blond youth said, 'we abandon the car and run in different directions. It will be for you to make your own way back to Le Donjon. The Colonel will take care of you.'

'So I am to be posted back? A returned empty?'

'You are blaming yourself? There is no reason to do so. Training can teach you how to kill. It cannot nerve you to pull the trigger. That comes only with experience.'

Seeing him now, at close quarters, she realised that he was older than she had thought. Older and much more formidable. 'You are Michel,' she said. It was a statement, not a question.

'I go by that name. And since it was I who asked London to send you, it was naturally my duty to look after you. Not,' he added, 'by any means an unpleasant duty.'

She let this go. It was not a moment for small talk. Rigby wanted the truth, however unpalatable.

'So I was sent to provoke Claudette into declaring her true feelings?'

'Correct. We could not move until we knew where she stood. Her father, you understand, was a most respected figure. It would have been inconceivable to have condemned her without the clearest proof. Which you obtained for us with considerable skill.'

'I might have done better,' said Rigby stiffly, 'if you had seen fit to take me into your confidence.'

'It is the unbreakable rule. Tell no one anything they do not need to know. And see how well things have fallen out. Gaston will talk. It will be learned that Claudette was killed by a female agent from London. No reprisals will fall on our organisation.'

'I'm glad you're satisfied.'

73

'More than satisfied. And might I predict that when you have had more experience you will be a very successful operator? For you possess the one faculty that counts above all others. An instinct for danger. It led you to leave the *camion* and take to your heels. If you had not done so you would be dead, or captured. The crossing of the bridge at Varenne had been sold to the Germans.'

'By that Belgian?'

'Correct. He did so to gain their tolerance for his trade. The Germans were aiming to kill the driver. He was one of our best men. The machine-gun is an indiscriminate weapon. The Belgian was killed too. If he had not been, we should, of course, have executed him ourselves.'

As the car started she was conducting an internal debate. The compliment he had paid to her was very agreeable. Should she tell him that it was based on a total misconception planted by the Colonel, who probably assumed that any well-dressed male in Le Donjon was a member of the Gestapo?

It would be honourable to confess this and she was on the point of doing so when a further thought stopped her. After all, he *didn't need* this information.

When she laughed Michel heard her, above the rattle of the car, and asked her what was amusing her.

She said, 'I'm just beginning to understand the rules.'

GOOD OLD MONTY

Jonathan and Sebastian were two hopeful young sharks. The sea they swam in stretched from Temple Bar to Aldgate Pump. It was full of reefs and pits, and currents which set in unexpected directions, and there were other sharks cruising about in it, older, heavier and more savage. So far they had managed to survive.

They had started with £5,000 each, the gift, in both cases, of aunts who had left it to them by will, coupled with the expression of a hope that they would put it to good use. The aunts were both believing Christians and it is possible that their idea of good differed from that of their nephews.

This joint fighting fund had grown over the past two years, more as a result of luck than judgement, or perhaps a little of both. They had stagged the Bryanstone issue, and had got into and out of International Cables at exactly the right moment. They had lost money in the Planetarium Project, but more than recovered it in Moon Stores when the shares nearly doubled in value as the result of a takeover bid by their largest rivals. They now had almost £100,000 waiting in a high interest deposit account.

'Ripe and ready for action,' said Jonathan.

'But where do we go in?' said Sebastian. 'The market's pretty dull at the moment.'

'We might devote a little attention to Office Accessories and B.T.'

'B.T.?'

'Business Tabulators.'

'Oh, that lot,' said Sebastian. 'What's so special about them?'

This was always the way. The more Jonathan got worked up the more laid back Sebastian became. Jack Sprat and his wife.

'The successful business man,' said Jonathan, 'spends perhaps ten hours in his office every day and the other fourteen at home—but most of that is sleeping and eating—'

'And commuting.'

'Yes. And commuting. Well, that doesn't leave more than, say, a couple of hours to fill in, if that. So what does he really need. An armchair, a television set and a comfortable bed.'

'And a comfortable wife.'

'Certainly. But think what a lot of attractive accessories he can buy to brighten up those ten hours in his office. The modern business man doesn't just need a massive desk and a well-adjusted chair—'

'What he really needs is a well-adjusted secretary.'

Jonathan ignored this. He was up in the stratosphere.

'He can have a computer of his own, with a

Visual Display Unit. And if he finds it tiresome to read, he fits a moniscope which enlarges the text and brings it down on to his desk. He can have pocket calculators and desk top calculators, a digital diary and a data bank. His secretary can be equipped with a fax machine, a word processor or, failing that, an electric typewriter.'

'Do you ever see an ordinary typewriter these days?'

'You might find one in the V and A. And think of this. He can have a multi-lingual electric translator. If he wants to know what a Preference Share or a Debenture is in, say, Dutch or Arabic he just presses the button.'

'Stupendous,' said Sebastian. 'So what?'

'So we think very seriously about Office Accessories and B.T. Leaders in the field, and running neck and neck.'

'Cutting each other's throats.'

'Exactly.'

'Then why don't they amalgamate?'

'You took the words out of my mouth.' Jonathan had the Stock Exchange Year Book open. He said, 'Nominal Capital, in both cases, five million. B.T. two million Ordinary issued and subscribed. One million Preference.'

'*Preferente aandelen?*'

'What are you talking about?'

'Just showing you that I knew the Dutch for Preference Shares.'

'Keep your eye on the ball, please. Office Accessories much the same. One million five hundred thousand Ordinary. No Preference.'

'So,' said Sebastian, who really had been attending, 'since both shares are standing a few points above par, either of them could take over the other *without increasing their Nominal Capital.* Their fingers must be itching.'

'Right. But *which* lot of fingers are itching most?'

The two young men looked at each other. The single table, at which they sat at opposite sides, and the floor round it were thick with copies of the *Financial Times,* which was the only newspaper they read.

'They're both holding their cards pretty close to their chests,' said Jonathan. 'You notice that they've neither of them published interim accounts. Maybe they're shy about this year's results.'

'It could have been a tough year,' agreed Sebastian. 'Eighteen months ago offices in the City were full of young men sitting on their bottoms all day fiddling with computers. That was when everyone was making money. Not now. Now a lot of them are on the street.'

'Right. And the last thing their company wants is more expensive office machinery. All the same, given good salesmanship they could have made a lot of money with those fancy lines.'

'We'll know as soon as the annual accounts are published.'

'No good. We must know sooner. When everyone knows it will be too late to do anything effective.'

'Do you think your Miranda might be able to help us?'

'For God's sake,' said Jonathan, 'she's only a typist at Accessories. Not the boss's right hand girl.'

'All the same she must know if they're getting keyed up for the A.G.M.

Both companies were legally obliged to hold their Annual General Meetings before the end of October. They would, no doubt, delay them as long as possible, but the Companies Act compelled them to give their shareholders at least twenty-one days' notice, along with the accounts and, in most cases, a statement by the Chairman.

'What we really want,' said Sebastian, 'is a reliable crystal ball. Failing that, I'll get round and make a few enquiries. You lush up Miranda and see if she can help.'

Jonathan accordingly spent his evenings standing Miranda expensive dinners whilst Sebastian passed his lunch hours in Panto's Sandwich Bar, off Cannon Street; where, if you listened hard, you could pick up more information about companies than you could on the floor of the Stock Exchange.

They met three days later to pool their

information.

'I haven't got a lot out of Miranda,' said Jonathan. 'She's quite willing to help, but at the moment all she gets is general office gossip. One straw in the wind. There's been no announcement about the annual bonus. So maybe things aren't so good. But here's a gleam of sunshine. The boss's regular secretary has been ordered off work by her medico. She goes at the end of the week and it's been suggested that Miranda might stand in for her. It doesn't mean that she'll get anything top secret, but she's bound to pick up a few valuable crumbs.'

'Sounds hopeful,' said Sebastian. 'I've been concentrating on the managements. B.T. has got what you might call a run-of-the-mill board. All been at the job for a long time. Maybe too long. Accessories is quite different. A number of young directors and a couple of real packywhatsits at the top.'

'I fancy the word you were looking for is pachyderms. But go on. This is interesting.'

'The Chairman is Colonel Melhuish. His number two is Major Messenger. The tone of the outfit is strictly regimental. They actually address each other as "Colonel" and "Major".'

'They can't be as old as all that.'

'Melhuish just scraped in, in the last months of the war. He was one of Montgomery's liaison officers. They both reached their

80

present ranks in the T.A. That doesn't worry them. No, sir. For them the war is still on. If any important decision has to be made, the question is, *"What would Monty have done?"'*

'For Christ's sake,' said Jonathan. Like all young men he despised the generation ahead of him. That someone old enough to have been his grandfather was still active in the City was a joke, in rather poor taste. 'So what do the rest of the board do?'

'Search me. Actually they're quite a bright crowd. One of them's got a Harvard business degree, one was in furniture design and two started in International Electronics. But the point is that they're junior officers. Their job is to say, "Yes, sir. No, sir", and stand up when spoken to.'

'It doesn't sound to me like the sort of board to cope with a real crisis. And we don't want to guess wrong.'

Their experience with Moon Stores had taught them the facts of City life. The immediate result of a takeover bid being announced was always the same. The shares of the to-be-taken over company went up. The shares of the taker-over went down.

'Only temporarily, of course,' said Jonathan. 'If the taker-over is big enough to swallow and digest the smaller company, its shares will go up again. Maybe right up. But not until it's shown that it hasn't bitten off more than it can chew.'

'I once saw a photograph,' said Sebastian, 'of a boa constrictor who'd swallowed a goat. He'd got it half-way down and he looked *most* uncomfortable.'

Jonathan was too deep in his own thoughts to worry about boa constrictors.

He said, 'The first step, clearly, is to put our money into Accessories. If they really have had a bad year, so much the better. They'll be ripe for being taken over. The shares will shoot up and we can sell when we think they are at the top. On the other hand, if we were wrong and they've been doing well, then they'll be the takers-over and we get out like lightning, before they've begun to dip.'

'Aren't you forgetting,' said Sebastian coldly, 'that there's another player in the game? The Stock Exchange. They'll have been thinking on exactly the same lines as us and they'll see the accounts as soon as we do. The Share and Loan Department will mark the shares down, as a precaution, *before the market opens.* What we've got to do is find out about those accounts in advance. How are we going to do that?'

'Keep our fingers crossed,' said Jonathan, 'and wait.'

They did not have to wait long.

It was Miranda who brought the news. She said, 'You wanted to know about those accounts, didn't you?'

'We certainly did.'

'Well, they've been arguing about them all week.'

'About what's in them?' said Jonathan hopefully.

'No. About who's to print them. I heard it all, because I'm now in what they call the Orderly Room. It's a tiny place, behind their office. I wonder why they call it that. Do you suppose it's a hint to me to keep it tidy?'

'It's a military term,' said Jonathan. 'Tell us about the printing.'

'Well, our printing's usually done by a small outfit called Williams and Davy. They hang out in Cork Street, off Bunhill Row. I had to take them a letter once and Mr Davy showed me round. They've got about half a dozen men working in the print shop. One old boy who looked as if he'd been there since the Boer War. The others were a lot younger.'

'And the argument was whether they could be trusted to handle the accounts?'

'Right. They'd always done them before, but Mr Messenger—the Major, that is—wanted them to go, this time, to a firm of security printers—whatever that means.'

'People who print share certificates and warrants and things like that. Very efficient and totally secure.'

'The Colonel said no, stick to the old firm. Apparently that was something General Montgomery had taught him. Don't desert your old friends just because someone more flashy turns up. But, he said, we'll make sure Davy understands how important security is. He must give the whole job to one reliable man. Me, I didn't see how he could do that. He'd have to print two thousand copies. Surely that would involve a lot of different people.'

'In the old days, perhaps,' said Jonathan thoughtfully. 'Not now. Not necessarily. Did you get any idea who might be given the actual job?'

'If I'd had to guess, I'd have said the old boy who sat by himself in the corner. He was almost buried under different machines. Only thing is, I wouldn't have put him in the top class for discretion.'

'Oh. Why not?'

'I thought he had a real drinker's face. Red nose, rum buds and all.'

'You can't always go by the colour of the nose,' said Jonathan. He spoke absently. His thoughts were far ahead.

He said, 'Here's where we need professional help. Smedley's the best man.'

Five days later Captain Smedley, who was the head of Temple Bar Detectives, gave Jonathan a verbal report. He said, 'The man you had your eye on is a Herbert Warburton. He's an experienced operator and, yes, he could do the job single-handed. He'd be given a handwritten copy of the Report and Accounts. He'd have a laser printer, a

84

terminal with a keyboard and an NP 402 photocopier. He'd type the stuff out on the keyboard. The tape would be fed into the laser printer which would produce four pages of A4. They'd be separate pages, but no problem. When they're put through the photocopier it will turn out the necessary numbers of folded four page documents. The envelopes are ready. He puts them in himself and takes them down to one of the big central post offices. They'd be on everyone's tables at breakfast time next morning.'

Jonathan thought about it, prodding it to see whether there were any holes in it. He said, 'I suppose a copy would be kept in the office.'

'Possibly. In the boss's safe. But his instructions to Warburton would be to put the manuscript copy through the shredder and to wipe the tape.'

It seemed foolproof. As long as Warburton played the game.

As though reading his thoughts Captain Smedley said, 'Yes, we thought about that. My men kept Warburton under observation for three days. His nose was a misleading signal. He turned out to be a teetotaller. He spent a good deal of time in milk bars and soft-drinks establishments. I began to get complaints from my men. Not the sort of place they normally frequent. So, having fallen down there, we made tentative approaches to one of the younger men, a youth who had been made redundant and was working out his notice. He was quite willing to help—at a price—but we soon discovered that he knew nothing about this particular job and the precautions being taken made it most unlikely that he'd be able to find anything out. So we reverted to Warburton. He had seemed unpromising, however—'

'However,' said Jonathan hopefully.

'Alcoholism isn't man's only vice. Warburton, it appears, is a gambler. Horses and dogs. As it happened both my men were on the job yesterday evening—one was relieving the other—at the moment when Warburton came out. A car drove up, he was bundled into it and driven off. My men followed discreetly. The chase ended in a quiet side street near the Oval. Warburton was dumped on the pavement and sat there, looking dazed. My men saw their chance. As soon as the other men—bookmakers' bullies they reckoned—had driven off, they picked up Warburton and whisked him into the back room of a nearby pub. He may have been a teetotaller, but when he was offered a large glass of brandy, he downed it like a man. From which point the entente developed quickly. It was what they had thought. He was nearly £800 in debt to his bookmaker and had just had a first warning of what to expect if he didn't pay up. When he was asked if he could

86

get hold of a copy of the Report and Accounts some days in advance and if he would hand them over for a thousand smackers, in cash, he couldn't say "yes" quick enough.'

'A thousand,' said Sebastian thoughtfully when he was told. 'And we've got Smedley's bill as well. That'll be at least another five hundred.'

'Worth it,' said Jonathan. 'If we can once get a preview of the accounts we're sitting pretty. If they're bad, and suggest a takeover by B.T. our shares go up. If they're good, we can get out bloody quick, before they start angling for B.T. and their shares go down.'

'And when they have gone down, we can buy in again.'

'If the takeover looks like working.'

'All right,' said Sebastian. 'Green light for Captain Smedley.'

When, two days later, a smudged but legible copy of the Report and Accounts arrived, their message came over loud and clear. A nasty loss on trading, covered by a transfer from reserves which weakened a weak balance sheet still further. The Chairman's report was a cry for help.

'Lovely,' said Jonathan. 'As soon as B.T. read this they'll start making takeover noises and Accessories' shares go up. Every point they go up is a thousand pounds in our pocket. We must give Miranda a very special dinner.'

87

'You, not me,' said Sebastian. 'I've got to lush up my girl for a change. She's been complaining of lack of attention lately.'

Miranda had brought one other item of news. The A.G.M. had been fixed for October 28th. 'That means the accounts must go out tomorrow evening,' said Jonathan. 'Just the right moment for a celebration.'

They celebrated over an expensive dinner and continued the celebration in Jonathan's flat. Miranda was as satisfactory as a bed mate as she had been as a spy.

Jonathan had rolled over and was settling himself for sleep when she said, 'I forgot to tell you. A funny thing happened when I was leaving the office this evening.'

'Wassat?' said Jonathan sleepily.

I'd left my bag behind and I nipped back to fetch it. The Colonel's office was empty. I went through it, to my little cubbyhole, picked up the bag and was starting back when I heard the two old boys coming. The Colonel must have gone along to have a word with the Major—his office is just down the passage. They were both laughing as they came along. The Colonel said, "That was a real minor operation," and the Major said, "It was terrific—" and then they saw me.'

When she stopped, Jonathan, who had only half been listening, sat up in bed. He said, 'Go on. What happened?'

'Nothing actually happened. It was the look
88

on the Colonel's face. As if he'd caught a spy and was going to have him shot. I was scared, for a moment. Then, thank God, I heard old Mrs Parkin rattling her pail and brushes. I said, "Good night," and made for the door. Neither of them said a word. They just looked at me.'

Jonathan said, 'Let's have it again. Exactly what the Colonel said.'

'He said, "That was a real minor operation." The Major agreed with him. It was what they were laughing so much about. They were both terrifically bucked—until they saw me.'

'Until they saw you,' said Jonathan slowly. 'Well, whatever it meant, we can't do any more about it tonight. Go to sleep.'

Miranda may have slept. Jonathan stayed awake until the first grey light of morning was creeping into the room. He dozed for an hour then.

Miranda cooked breakfast. Whilst they were eating it, she said, 'I don't really want to go back to the office.'

'You must,' said Jonathan. 'If you stay away they'll know you heard something you shouldn't have done. There'll be other people about. They won't start anything.'

His own office hours were irregular. He thought he'd take a walk and do some solid thinking. Not a walk in the country, with cows and road-hogs. A walk in the City among sensible people who thought about money.

Bishopsgate, Houndsditch, Aldgate, Fenchurch Street, Lombard Street, Threadneedle Street.

Think, boy, think.

What was meant by a minor operation and why had the Colonel spoken about it in the way he did? Surely it would have been more natural for him to have said, 'It was *only* a minor operation, but it was successful.' Instead, they had referred to it as though it was a major operation.

Halfway down Aldgate he started thinking about 'minor'. Might it have been 'miner'? A digging operation. It opened a new line of thought, but didn't take him very far. Opposite the Bank of England a rather disturbing thought occurred to him. Might it have been a 'mina' operation. A mina bird, he remembered, could be taught to talk and repeat things back. Had they been using Miranda as a mina bird, telling her things which they knew she'd repeat? This was such an alarming idea that he quickened his pace and went round the whole circuit again, finishing outside his own office, two rooms on a top floor in Alderman's Walk.

Sebastian had left a note, *Off with Jeannie tonight. Great hopes.* He knew exactly what Sebastian was hoping for. Jeannie was a Scots girl with a dour character and a beautiful body. He wished him good luck, relocked the office and made for a restaurant where he could find a good high tea. By six o'clock he was home, sitting in his untidy living room, still thinking.

He decided to approach the problem from a different angle.

So far he had been wondering what the Colonel had meant and why it had seemed to him to be important. All right. Now, for a change, try to work out why it had seemed so significant to him, Jonathan. As it had done. It had made him sit up in bed. It had rung a bell. Something he had read somewhere.

This thought narrowed the field dramatically because, apart from the Stock Exchange Year Book, he didn't read a lot. Lately it had been books about the war. Not the 1939–45 War. His father and his uncle had bored him stiff yacking about that. No. The First World War. And not the war in the trenches, which had been a bloody shambles, but some of the interesting and picturesque outside shows.

Lights were springing up all round. You're on the right track now. Keep thinking.

He got up and looked at the clutter of books in the shelf beside the fire. And, by God, there it was. In front of his eyes.

He grabbed the book, leafed through the index to the letter 'M', turned back to the passage indicated and read it through. He had found what the Colonel was talking about. Then the reality of the position hit him.

It was seven o'clock. The Stock Exchange

had long shut up shop. Impossible to sell today and tomorrow would be too late. He had found the answer and was powerless to use it.

Being given to extravagant gestures he was on the point of relieving his fury and frustration by hurling the book through the window when another thought occurred to him. Perhaps it was not too late. Accessories' shares were quoted on both the London and the New York Stock Exchange. If he was going to do it, he would have to be quick. No chance of consulting Sebastian. He would have to take the full responsibility.

He grabbed the telephone and started to dial.

*   *   *

On the following morning he reached the office at ten o'clock, beating Sebastian by a short head. Sebastian's face was as red as if it had been slapped. He was carrying two lots of papers, which he slammed down on the desk.

He said, 'In case you're interested, those are the accounts of Accessories and B.T. Both arrived this morning.'

Jonathan toyed with the documents for a moment, but made no attempt to read them.

'Go on. Help yourself to an eyeful. Accessories on top of the world. Good trading results, excellent reserves. B.T. on its uppers, almost begging to be taken over. And we paid that old shit Warburton a thousand smackers for a phoney set of accounts.' The thought seemed to choke him. 'All we can do is see if we can offload our Accessories' shares before they go down too far. Well, don't sit there like a bloody idol, say something.'

'I was waiting till you'd finished,' said Jonathan placidly. 'There's one excellent reason why we can't sell Accessories. I sold the whole lot yesterday evening through New York. They were actually a bit up on what we paid for them. Not quite enough to cover our expenses, but nearly.'

Sebastian stared at him.

'I realised, at the last moment, what the Colonel was talking about. It was a Meiner operation. M-e-i-n-e-r. Short for Meinertzhagen, who was on Allenby's Intelligence Staff in the Palestine Campaign. T.E. Lawrence actually refers to him in that way in *The Seven Pillars of Wisdom*. Look. *Meiner thought out false papers, elaborate and confidential.* That was what I'd read and it must have stuck in my mind. Allenby wanted to persuade the Turks that he was going to attack on the left, while actually he was going in on the right. So Meinertzhagen rode out between the lines, was spotted, turned tail and bolted. Carefully dropping his haversack in the process. Full of misleading information. Exactly what they pulled on us. A Meiner operation.'

Sebastian let out his breath in one long whistle.

'Thank the Lord you spotted it in time,' he said. 'This calls for a celebration. I'll book a table for four at the Savoy.'

'From which I gather,' said Jonathan, 'that you, too, had a successful evening.'

*   *   *

The Colonel and the Major were also celebrating.

'Jolly good show,' said the Colonel.

'A real haversack ruse,' said the Major. 'Monty did the same thing before Alamein.'

'That chap Warburton must have made a fortune. I wonder how many times he sold those phoney accounts. Almost everyone who was interested seems to have got their hands on them.'

'I believe he was asking a thousand a time at the end.'

'Effective, anyway. Stopped any last minute selling.'

'I believe one small packet was sold, in New York.'

'You know what Monty said. You can't trust the Yanks.'

'Good old Monty.'

NO PLACE LIKE HOME

From our point of view the Italian Campaign was a regulated advance. Regulated that is to say, by the Germans. Geography was on their side. Italy is a narrow country, full of mountains, which slow up the infantry and mostly prevent the passage of any transport less mobile than a mule.

In such conditions the anti-tank gun and the machine-gun were important, but the mine was king.

The mine has always been a favourite German toy (elder brother to that industry which turns out clockwork clowns and the finest fireworks in the world). And the German habit, in retreat is to leave plenty of souvenirs behind.

There was the mine which would remove your foot when you trod on it, another which blew off your wheel if you ran over it, and an even more powerful one which destroyed the track of your tank. There was the mine which jumped in the air like a jack-in-the-box and went off in your face.

There was the delayed action mine. There was the dummy mine laid in the road with the real mine in the hedge at just the point where you would be likely to make a diversion. And there was the double mine, the first near the surface and asking to be lifted: the other much deeper, and attached to the first with a contraption which sent it off when the top one was moved.

Nor must it be imagined that mines were the business only of sappers and a few front-line infantry. All arms and all ranks were made forcibly aware of them. (A distinguished Corps Commander, who subsequently became CIGS, will give testimony to the truth of what I write.)

I was at the time Battery Captain of F Division, and my job was the simple but interesting one of feeding and maintaining two hundred men and bringing up to them a wide range of necessities from petrol and oil and ammunition, down to bars of chocolate and mail. And since the various dumps and echelons and stores from which these things came were moving almost as fast at one end as the recipients were at the other, it involved a fair amount of getting about.

I have no intention of painting it up as a hard and dangerous job. Compared with what others were doing it was neither. But it was interesting and varied and the most deeply satisfying job that I have ever done in my life. That by the way I did, however, certainly become mine-conscious.

I did most of my journeying by Jeep. And one afternoon in, I think, late July (but I may be a few weeks out either way: that summer remains one sunny, dusty, turbulent whole in my memory) I was sitting beside the road on the Eastern shore of Lake Trasimene, eating my haversack ration and watching an Italian peasant at work in the field. Since that part of the countryside had been the scene of tank fighting in the past 24 hours and was probably still within long artillery range of the enemy, I could not help admiring such devotion to agriculture.

He was a sturdy old boy, as brown and tough looking as a boot, and he was engaged in hoeing.

In that part of the country, where land is precious, the farmer plants his vines in close rows, and in the margin of the turned earth at their foot may grow vegetables also, with long strips of grazing between the rows. As I watched he was moving carefully along the outer 'strip', which lay next to the road. And suddenly I picked up my glasses to watch him more closely.

Having hoed for a few yards, he stopped, picked up his stick—a shoulder-high shepherd's crook—and advanced slowly, waving the stick in front of him, in slow circles like a wand. Having apparently satisfied himself that all was well, he laid down his stick to mark the limit of his advance, returned, picked up his hoe, and hoed up to the stick.

He had performed this ritual three times before I grasped what it was all about. Then I

97

got up and walked cautiously across to see more.

I was close enough to observe every detail of what followed. The waving stick halted suddenly then dipped just as a dowser's twig will stiffen and dip. The man laid his stick aside, got down on to his knees, and grubbed about with his hands in the edge of the vines.

Then he lifted out an Italian type anti-personnel mine. I knew what it was as soon as I saw it. We'd found a batch of them in our last harbour, and they had cost me a lorry driver.

'Pericoloso,' I said. 'Mines. Molto pericoloso.'

He grinned amiably at me and pointed back along the hedge. I could count six all carefully unearthed and stacked in full view.

At that moment a Jeep with RE signs on it squealed to a halt and the Sapper officer who was driving it got out. He was an old friend of mine.

'Just look what I've found, Jack,' I said. 'A one-man mine disposal unit. Do your stuff. Giuseppe. Go on. Ancora.'

Giuseppe grinned again and picked up his stick. Five yards on, in the verge, he found two more mines. Anti-vehicle ones this time. They must have been planted in conjunction with the blown culvert just up the road to catch a diversion (only fortunately the culvert had been so inefficiently blown that a diversion had not been necessary).

'This is terrific,' said Jack. 'Do you realise what these are? They're the new plastic mines. The ones our detectors won't detect.'

I saw the force of this at once. We had got quite efficient mine detectors. You swept them about over the surface and when they passed over metal they went 'ping.' And you stopped and did some digging. Sometimes it was an old kettle, but quite often it was a mine.

Now the Germans had taken to laying mines without any metal parts at all, mostly made of plastic. In the end we got a detector which would deal with them, too, but meanwhile they were causing a lot of casualties.

While I was thinking Jack had been working things out.

'Ask him,' he said, 'if he'd like to earn a lot of money. Good pay. Good food.'

Giuseppe said he had plenty of good food at home and money didn't interest him.

'Appeal to his patriotism,' said Jack. 'These types are always saying they want to get their own back on the Tedesci. Now's his chance.'

I appealed to his patriotism, but in vain.

Jack played his last card. He took from his pocket a brand new crisp unopened packet of cigarettes. English cigarettes. Giuseppe's eyes lit up at once.

'Tell him,' said Jack impressively, 'that I will deposit five hundred—five hundred—

cigarettes at his farm now. And he shall have fifty a day as long as he works for us.'

The internal struggle was short, but of terrible intensity. To say that cigarettes were worth their weight in gold in Italy that summer is actually a slight underestimate of their value.

'He says he'll think about it,' I reported. 'He lives in that white house over there. I think he's weakening.'

Knowing Jack as a resourceful officer, I felt certain he'd get his man. But it was three weeks later, and nearly a hundred miles further north before I saw him again, and was able to inquire about my protege.

'Giuseppe?' said Jack. 'Yes. That was a funny thing. We persuaded him to come along, in the end. He upped the price to a thousand cigarettes before he'd move, but once he got going he was willing enough. Came out with us on patrol, crook and all. The only thing was, it wouldn't work.'

'Wouldn't work?'

'So he said. He said it was all right, at home, in his own fields. But up in the front line he was afraid. And when he was afraid his instinct, or whatever it was, wouldn't function. After he'd led us slap through a couple of minefields we let him go.'

'Do you think he was telling the truth?'

'My own idea,' said Jack, 'is that he was a fraud from beginning to end. What could be easier than to buy a few mines and wait till some intelligent officer was watching you and pretend to find them. Net profit a thousand cigarettes.'

'I don't believe it,' I said. 'Too subtle. I think his own explanation was the right one. He'd got a genuine instinct, but it wouldn't function under fire.'

I suppose the only way to have made sure would have been to have gone back to Lake Trasimene to see if we could catch him trying it on someone else. But we had other things to do that summer.

ST ETHELBURGA AND THE ANGEL OF DEATH

(MUSIC. HELD BEHIND)

ANNOUNCER: Mr Behrens and Mr Calder belong to a very secret organisation headed by Mr Fortescue—an organisation even more secret, and apparently more deadly, than the celebrated M.I.5.

FORTESCUE: My shoulders are reasonably broad Calder. I am well accustomed to being blamed by our political masters for things for which I have no responsibility at all. But in this case, I am not sure that there is not substratum—a mere substratum—of justification for the criticism.

CALDER: How do you make that out, Sir? All countries have got neo-Nazis. Or the equivalent—

FORTESCUE: (<u>Patient</u>) I am not talking about neo-Nazis, Calder. They form a lunate fringe in every western democracy. The criticism, in this case, is that

	they are receiving support, and money, from actual Nazi war criminals who have fled to this country—with their ill-gotten loot. Criminals whom we have not troubled to hunt out.
BEHRENS:	Because we don't know where they are.
FORTESCUE:	(<u>Still patient</u>) Naturally, Behrens, naturally. If we knew they were there we would do something at once. But the fact that we cannot immediately identify them is *not* regarded as an adequate excuse. It has not stopped our West German allies from hunting down more than five hundred war criminals and bringing them before the Courts. The Israeli authorities have scored notable successes in this field. The C.I.A. has rounded up more than a dozen in the Americas. We, and we alone, are accused of dragging our feet.
CALDER:	Is there any reason to suppose that there *are* any notable Nazi war criminals in this country?
FORTESCUE:	Previously—the contingency was, perhaps, remote. Now, I think a prima facie case has

	been made out.
CALDER:	You mean this paper they found when they raided that meeting. Is there any reason to suppose it's genuine?
FORTESCUE:	There are two reasons. The strenuous efforts which were made to destroy it. And the fact that the message itself was in a wartime German cipher. A cipher, may I add, which was used exclusively by high-level party and police officials.
	It was a single, much faded and folded, sheet of paper. When decoded, it said, 'If you require further funds or assistance in grave emergency, suggest you approach Saint Ethelburga of Seahampton'. This was followed by a sketch representing the Angel of Death.
BEHRENS:	Good heavens Fleischmann!
FORTESCUE:	Yes, Behrens, Fleischmann. The man universally known, in Nazi circles, as the Angel of Death— Dr Konrad Fleischmann. The doctor who, by the end of the war, was directing Hitler's extermination programe. I believe you met him, Behrens?

BEHRENS:	I never actually met him. I heard a good deal about him. He wasn't a German you know. He was a Pole. You remember, after the partition of 1939, Hitler invited any Poles with medical qualifications to come across and work for the Reich. Not many accepted. Fleischmann was one who did. He was a clever young man. He cured Dr Goebbels of a painful skin disease. After that he never looked back.
FORTESCUE:	A Polish national, maybe. But he was born in South East London.
BEHRENS:	Yes, I always understood that he spent the first ten years of his life in Clapham. He went back to Poland with his parents after the '14-18 war. And came back here again in the thirties to complete his medical training.
FORTESCUE:	You can see how this background and upbringing lend support to the idea that Fleischmann might have slipped across here in 1945. And could have been living here quietly ever since.

CALDER:	Bit like looking for a needle in a hay-stack, isn't it?
FORTESCUE:	Maybe, but we have discovered that St Ethelburga's Southampton is a preparatory school.
CALDER:	A school?
FORTESCUE:	Investigation seemed to be indicated. Through the good offices of the Seahampton Bank Manager, who keeps the school account and is an old friend of mine, I have secured a post for *you*, Calder.
CALDER:	Me? Behrens would be much better at that sort of thing.
FORTESCUE:	No doubt. Unfortunately I had little choice. Subjects which the new man was required to teach included rugby football and judo.
CALDER:	Oh!
FORTESCUE:	The Headmaster is a Mr Pellumpton. Him you can dismiss from your investigations. He taught at the school before the war, and had a creditable war-time career in the Royal Artillery. Term begins the day after tomorrow.

(FADE OUT:-)

106

(<u>FADE IN ON</u>:-)

MR PELLUMPTON:	I'm sure you'll get on famously here, Calder—apart from games and judo, I have you down for Senior Arithmetic. You can manage that?
CALDER:	Er—yes Headmaster. I should think so.
MR PELLUMPTON:	Junior forms in History, Geography, English and, of course, Religious Knowledge. Do you know any Biology?
CALDER:	Very little, I'm afraid.
MR PELLUMPTON:	Perhaps you could manage intermediate Biology. Personally, I think it's a mistake. Simply puts ideas into their heads. Incidentally—your dog, I hope he'll be quite happy in the cricket pavilion. We don't use it in the Autumn term, you see.
CALDER:	Oh, perfectly. Rasselas is a very adaptable dog.
MR PELLUMPTON:	(<u>Moving to window and opening it</u>) He seems to have made friends already. He's no savage, I hope?
CALDER:	No, gentle as a lamb. Who are those two boys playing with him?

MR PELLUMPTON:	David Rawnsley and Michael Meldrum. Both in their last term here. Nice boys, but they need a bit of firmness. The other boys are apt to follow their lead. Be firm with those two and you'll have no trouble with the others.
CALDER:	Thanks for the tip.
MR PELLUMPTON:	(At window) Matron—Matron—
CALDER:	Yes, Mr Pellumpton.
MR PELLUMPTON:	Could you come here a moment. (To Calder) Miss Martin, our Matron, a tower of strength.

(DOOR OPENING)

MR PELLUMPTON:	Oh, Matron. You haven't met Mr Calder yet.
MATRON:	How do you do. I've given you the room at the end of the corridor, beyond the music-room, Mr Calder.
MR PELLUMPTON:	Excellent. You should be very comfortable there.

(DOOR SHUTTING)

MR PELLUMPTON:	If there's anything you want, just ask Matron and she'll find

	it for you.
CALDER:	I'll bear that in mind, Headmaster.

(<u>FADE OUT</u>:-)

(<u>FADE IN ON BELL FOR END OF CLASS</u>)

CALDER:	All right, you can go.

(<u>A MAD SCRAMBLE FOR THE DOOR</u>)

CALDER:	All except you Meldrum and you, Rawnsley—close the door.

(<u>DOOR SHUTS AND CUTS DOWN THE NOISE</u>)

CALDER:	Now Medlrum and Rawnsley.
DAVID RAWNSLEY:	Yes, Sir?
CALDER:	I have to teach you the rudiments of mathematics, plane geometry and algebra, up to, but *not* beyond, quadratic equations. You have to be taught. And it occurs to me that we shall all find it easier if a reasonable standard of behaviour is maintained.
DAVID RAWNSLEY:	We're terribly reasonable, Sir.
CALDER:	Your last maths master, Mr Kellaway, didn't think so.

DAVID RAWNSLEY:	Oh. We didn't drive him mad you know. He was mad before he started.
CALDER:	Quite. I saw you two making friends with my dog.
DAVID RAWNSLEY:	Is he yours, Sir? He's *lovely*.
MICHAEL MELDRUM:	A wolf hound, isn't he?
CALDER:	He's a Persian deer hound. He'll be taking up residence in the cricket pavilion. Would you two care to look after him?
DAVID RAWNSLEY:	(<u>As if he can scarcely believe it</u>) Look *after* him?
CALDER:	Feed him and water him, and take him out for a run each day. I shan't have much time for that sort of thing myself.
DAVID RAWNSLEY:	That'd be absolutely super. Wouldn't it, Mike?
MICHAEL MELDRUM:	Terrific.
CALDER:	On one condition—
DAVID RAWNSLEY:	I thought there'd be a catch somewhere.
CALDER:	That you and Meldrum behave in *my* classes—you can do what you like in anyone elses —
DAVID RAWNSLEY:	It's a deal.
MICHAEL MELDRUM:	O.K.
CALDER:	Very well then, starting from now.

(<u>FADE OUT</u>:-)

110

(FADE IN ON:-)

MR APPLETON: Good morning. My name's Appleton. We haven't been properly introduced.

CALDER: I'm Calder.

MR APPLETON: (Doubtfully) I hope you'll be happy here. It takes a bit of getting used to.

CALDER: You've been at it for some time, I gather?

MR APPLETON: Yes. Yes, quite a time. You can't think how often I've had to complain about the tea in the break.

CALDER: It has got rather an odd taste.

MR APPLETON: I'm convinced that Cook doesn't warm the pot. You can't make good tea unless you warm the pot. It's those little things that count. If Pellumpton was married it's the sort of thing his wife would look after. As it is, it gets left to Matron. Miss Martin's a competent enough woman, but she can't function as house-keeper *and* matron. It's not to be expected. I'm afraid I shall have to ask you to be kind enough *not* to smoke in the Common Room.

111

CALDER:	Oh, sorry. I'm trying to cut down on it, actually.
MR APPLETON:	I suffer from very severe asthma. Cigarette smoke aggravates it.
CALDER:	(<u>Seeing his chance</u>) I sympathise with you. Now *I've* been having a good deal of trouble myself. Headaches, and a sort of stuffy feeling. I thought it might be something to do with sinuses?
MR APPLETON:	Very likely. My asthma seems to come on quite arbitrarily. There was an article I read about it which suggested that it had something to do with pollen, but I can get it just as badly in mid-winter.

(<u>FROM OUTSIDE WE BECOME CONSCIOUS OF SERGEANT TUCKETT KEEPING THE BOYS OCCUPIED IN FIRST BREAK. 'RUNNING ON THE SPOT. COMMENCE. ONE TWO. ONE TWO, ONE TWO. PICK UP THOSE KNEES THERE. COME ON. PICK 'EM UP. THEY DON'T WEIGH A TON. ONE TWO.</u>

ONE TWO. ONE TWO'.)

MR APPLETON:	Oh dear, I wonder if you'd very much mind closing the window.
CALDER:	(Doing so, and shutting out most of the noise) And who is that energetic character?
MR APPLETON:	That is Sergeant Tuckett. Pellumpton is old fashioned enough to believe in—physical jerks—I believe we used to call them. I shouldn't wish to be thought critical, but in my view the boys would be far better occupied in break if they were sitting down quietly and reading.

(FADE CUT:-)

(FADE IN ON THE TUNE, 'DANNY BOY' PLAYED WITH TWO HANDS AND SOME CONFIDENCE).

MR ABIGAIL:	Rawnsley, keep the rhythm going. That's not too bad. Firmness on the down beat. Turn—tum, tum—tum—TUM te tum.

(AS IT REACHES THE TOP

113

NOTE ON THE FIFTH LINE, 'OF—DANNY—BOY—' RECEIVES AN UNEXPECTED ACCOMPANIMENT OF SENTIMENTAL HOWLING

MR ABIGAIL: Good heavens! What's that?

RAWNSLEY: I think it's Mr Calder's dog, Sir.

MR ABIGAIL: (<u>At window</u>) Go away. Shoo! We're doing very nicely without you.
(<u>DOOR</u>)

CALDER: I'm so sorry. That's Rasselas. He can't resist joining in. Rasselas! Pipe down, for goodness sake. I'm so sorry he disturbed you.

MR ABIGAIL: We had finished.

(<u>DISTANT BELL</u>)

MR ABIGAIL: There's the bell. You'd better run along, Rawnsley.

RAWNSLEY: Yes, Sir, thank you, Sir.

CALDER: (<u>As the boy goes</u>) We haven't met, have we? My name's Calder.

MR ABIGAIL: Abigail. I teach music here.

CALDER: You're not one of the resident

114

	staff, then?
MR ABIGAIL:	No. No. Not at all. I live in the town. I teach at quite a number of the schools round here.
CALDER:	That must be very pleasant. Have you been doing it for long?
MR ABIGAIL:	I came down to Seahampton— for my health—shortly after the war. The air here is said to be particularly bracing. It's certainly very cold in winter and I'm afraid the heating system here is sadly out of date.
CALDER:	That won't do my sinuses any good.
MR ABIGAIL:	You suffer from sinus trouble?
CALDER:	Chronically. (Hopefully) I wonder if you happen to know a good remedy for it?
MR ABIGAIL:	I had an aunt who suffered terribly from her sinuses. In the end, she had them—I believe the word was—'opened'. It sounded rather drastic.
CALDER:	Was it effective?
MR ABIGAIL:	She died very shortly after, something else you understand, so it was difficult to say.

(<u>FADE OUT</u>:-)

(<u>FADE IN ON FEET ON
WOODEN FLOOR</u>:-)

CALDER: A lovely morning, Sergeant.

TUCKETT: Beautiful. Lovely air down here. Fill your lungs with it. (<u>Does so</u>)

CALDER: We haven't met yet. My name's Calder.

TUCKETT: You'd be the new mathematics master. To take poor Mr Kellaway's place.

CALDER: That's right. Apparently I'm to teach judo as well. I've promised to give Rawnsley and Meldrum some private tuition this afteroon.

TUCKETT: That's a pair of young tearabouts for you. A spell in the ranks would do 'em both good.

CALDER: You were in the Army yourself, of course, Sergeant?

TUCKETT: First Hampshire's. Joined as a band-boy. Right through the late war. Finished as a Sergeant. Were you in the war, Sir?

CALDER: I had a rather—varied—wartime career. My health wasn't always the best.

116

TUCKETT:	(<u>Scornfully</u>) That was bad luck.
CALDER:	I've suffered since I was a boy, from blocked sinuses.
TUCKETT:	Sinuses, eh?
CALDER:	I've been to a number of different doctors; they've tried but none of them has really been able to achieve much.
TUCKETT:	Doctors! You don't want to bother with doctors. All they're useful for is screwing you down, and signing the certificate. What you want to do is to breathe in—deep. Fill your lungs. Then breathe out, slowly. That'll clear your sinuses better than any medicine.

(<u>FADE OUT ON THIS</u>)

(<u>FADE IN</u>)

MELDRUM:	O-O-O-W!
MATRON:	What a fuss.
MELDRUM:	It stings.
MATRON:	If it hurts you, it probably does you good. (<u>Door</u>) Good morning, Mr Calder.
CALDER:	Good morning, Matron. I've come to attend your sick parade.

117

MATRON:	And what's wrong with you?
CALDER:	I've got a splinter in my finger. I'm very bad at digging things out of myself.
MELDRUM:	(<u>going</u>) If you let her do it, she'll probably start by cutting the finger off.
MATRON:	That's quite enough from you, Meldrum. Off you go. That boy's getting too big for his boots. Just hold it out. It must have come off the gym floor.
CALDER:	Ouch!
MATRON:	There you are—you'll survive.
CALDER:	Yes. Do you know that's a thing that's struck me about St Ethelburga's. The way people survive and stay on here. Who's your oldest inhabitant—apart from the Head, I mean?
MATRON:	Both the gardeners were here before the war—I believe—and cook.
CALDER:	Yes. But the teaching staff?
MATRON:	Well, let me think. Mr Appleton—he came just after the war. So did Sergeant Tuckett. They're the only two real old-timers. The young men on the staff, they come for a term or two and go on somewhere else.

118

CALDER: What about Mr Abigail?
MATRON: Oh, yes. He's been about a good many years. I wasn't counting him, being just a visiting master. Were *you* thinking of making this a permanent post?
CALDER: I was toying with the idea.

(<u>BELL IN DISTANCE</u>)

CALDER: Goodness. Eleven o'clock already. I'm meant to be teaching the fifth form geography—

(<u>FADE OUT</u>:-)

(<u>FADE IN ON</u>:-)

FORTESCUE: —So that is the score, up to date, Behrens. A Mr Appleton, who appeared on the staff in 1946 and suffers from asthma. A bachelor. Quite a common name. No known connections. Next, there's Sergeant Tuckett—spelt with two 't's'. Joined the First Hampshires as a boy and served through the war. Two curious things about him. Calder happened to notice that the badge tattooed on his forearm was the regimental badge of the Lancashire Fusiliers.

BEHRENS: Seems odd. If he did *all* his service in the Hampshire's.

FORTESCUE: Very odd. The second point was that he seems to have a permanently crooked little finger. The sort of thing that might have happened years ago, when he was a boy, perhaps.

BEHRENS: It wouldn't have kept him out of the army. Not in 1939.

FORTESCUE: No. But it would feature in his medical history sheet, I imagine.

BEHRENS: Well, we can check that one easily enough.

FORTESCUE: Then finally, we have a Mr Abigail. He, too, has been around Seahampton since early 1946. He's a bachelor, and no one seems to know where he comes from. He is apparently an L.R.C.M. The College of Music might be able to give us a lead.

BEHRENS: I'll try them. Might we be able to tackle this from the other end, perhaps?

FORTESCUE:	The other end?
BEHRENS:	When young Fleischmann went over to the Germans in 1939 he certainly wasn't called Fleischmann. That's the name he adopted for his new career in the Reich. It occurred to me that if we could unearth from captured records what his original Polish name was, we'd have something to start on. He was born in England. His birth must have been registered at Somerset House.
FORTESCUE:	But suppose you could unearth his birth certificate—of what assistance would that be?
BEHRENS:	Well—we should know for certain when his birthday is. People sometimes change their names, but forget to change their birthdays.
FORTESCUE:	It seems to me to be a slender chance. I suppose it will be worth the effort.
BEHRENS:	It's going to *be* an effort. Most of the records we want are held by the Russians, and they're a bit short on co-operation just now.

(FADE OUT:-)

121

(<u>FADE IN ON</u>:-)

DAVID RAWNSLEY: —Well, Mr Prentise said, he was the last judo master, that if a man rushed at you with a knife, as he raised his right arm you grabbed his wrist, put your left foot forward, did a half turn and threw him over your left leg.

CALDER: Suppose he didn't raise his right arm?

DAVID RAWNSLEY: He'd have to, if he was going to stab you.

CALDER: Don't you believe it, Rawnsley. A real killer swings upwards— and usually left handed. Then the point of his knife goes *under* your ribs and *into* your heart.

MICHAEL MELDRUM: I suppose you were taught all this when you were being trained?

CALDER: (<u>Cautiously</u>) Trained?

DAVID RAWNSLEY: In the Secret Service.

CALDER: And whatever put it into your heads that I was in the Secret Service.

DAVID RAWNSLEY: My uncle.

CALDER: Who the devil's your uncle?

DAVID RAWNSLEY: Sir Andrew Charteris. He's in

	the Home Office. Do you know him?
CALDER:	(<u>Grimly</u>) Yes, I know him. He's the biggest chatterbox in Whitehall.
DAVID RAWNSLEY:	We thought we'd read something about you in the papers. When you gave evidence about the chap who was shot by the night-club owner. And when we mentioned Rasselas, he told us all about you.
CALDER:	I see. And I suppose you've told everybody?
DAVID RAWNSLEY:	No fear. It's much too good for them.
CALDER:	I didn't only mean the boys.
DAVID RAWNSLEY:	Then it *is* one of the staff you're after. I said it was.
MICHAEL MELDRUM:	And we can tell you which one it is.
CALDER:	I see. Well, that'll save me a lot of trouble. Which one is it?
MICHAEL MELDRUM:	Old Apples.
CALDER:	Mr Appleton.
DAVID RAWNSLEY:	That's right.
MICHAEL MELDRUM:	He keeps the stuff under his bed.
CALDER:	*What* stuff?
DAVID RAWNSLEY:	The loot. It's bank notes. He's got two suitcases full of them.

123

CALDER: You aren't making all this up, by any chance.

DAVID RAWNSLEY: Of course we aren't. We saw him.

CALDER: *How* did you see him?

MICHAEL MELDRUM: Well—

DAVID RAWNSLEY: Well—I suppose we might get into trouble if this was found out. So it had better remain confidential.

CALDER: Oh, certainly.

DAVID RAWNSLEY: We've found a way we can get up onto the roof at night. And Michael's got a telescope. His uncle gave it to him.

MICHAEL MELDRUM: The original idea was to do a bit of star gazing.

DAVID RAWNSLEY: Only that got boring, so we took to looking in at people's bedroom windows.

CALDER: Good God!

MICHAEL MELDRUM: Do you know Sergeant Tuckett wears a sort of corset, to keep his stomach in. We saw him taking it off.

DAVID RAWNSLEY: And Matron dyes her hair.

CALDER: I hope you didn't watch her undressing.

DAVID RAWNSLEY: We couldn't actually. Most of her room's out of sight. But we could see *right* into old Apple's room. And that's when we saw

124

	him pulling out this case and unlocking it—it had two different locks and keys—and taking out some bank notes—
CALDER:	What did he do with them?
MICHAEL MELDRUM:	He put them in his wallet. Four or five of them.
DAVID RAWNSLEY:	It's obvious, isn't it. He's done a big robbery and got away with the loot. But he's too crafty to splurge it round. So he just uses a bit here and there when he needs it.
CALDER:	What do you suppose he does spend it on?
DAVID RAWNSLEY:	He's always buying medicine for that old asthma of his. He slips out in break and gets it from the shop at the end of the drive. I've seen him.
CALDER:	Right. I think you really could be helpful here. Next time you see him going down to the shop, tip me the wink. (He hears the Head approaching) (Louder) Come on now. One more throw. It's your turn Meldrum.
MICHAEL MELDRUM:	How are the boys shaping, Calder?
CALDER:	I think they're both going to be *very* useful, Headmaster.

(<u>FADE OUT</u>:-)

(<u>FADE IN ON</u>:-)

(<u>SOUND OF DIALLING—
THEN RINGING TONE—
THEN CLICK OF
RECEIVER COMING OFF
(N.B. A TWO-ENDED
TELEPHONE
CONVERSATION</u>)

CALDER:	Behrens? Calder here. Anything for me yet?
BEHRENS:	(<u>Distort</u>) Hello Calder. Is this line safe?
CALDER:	I can't think why it shouldn't be. I'm speaking from the local pub. Unless maybe Pellumpton has it tapped to stop his boys putting bets on horses.
BEHRENS:	(<u>Distort</u>) They sound a wild lot.
CALDER:	They are. Did you check Sergeant Tuckett?
BEHRENS:	I did. The Hampshire's hadn't heard of him. But your idea about the Fusiliers was a good one. They lost a Sergeant *Blackett* in 1944. Details are all correct, tattoo mark, crooked finger and all.
CALDER:	When you say they lost him?

BEHRENS:	He deserted.
CALDER:	Tcht!
BEHRENS:	You're not going to do anything about it, are you?
CALDER:	Certainly not. Much too late. Probably covered by the amnesty anyway. I might drop him a hint that I know. If only to stop him lecturing the boys on esprit de corps and the team spirit. What about Appleton?
BEHRENS:	Ah! Now you're talking! When I showed that pound note to our friends in blue they really *were* excited. Do you remember the Cranston case?
CALDER:	Vaguely.
BEHRENS:	1944. Cranston was Head Cashier of the Ovaz Group. Their internal audit must have got a bit slack in war-time because he walked out with nearly ten thousand pounds in notes.
CALDER:	And this is one of them?
BEHRENS:	That's right. I had the top brass on the telephone demanding to know where I'd got it from.
CALDER:	Stall them for the moment. Tell them it's a security matter.
BEHRENS:	I don't think I can hold them off for long.

CALDER:	Twenty-four hours should do.

(<u>FADE OUT</u>:-)

(<u>FADE IN ON</u>:-)

(<u>A GENTLE KNOCKING</u>)

MR APPLETON:	(<u>Querulous</u>) Who is it?
CALDER:	Calder.
MR APPLETON:	Oh! One moment.

(<u>A SHUFFLING. THEN SOUND OF ROOM DOOR BEING UNLOCKED</u>)

MR APPLETON:	What is it?
CALDER:	Can I come in?
MR APPLETON:	I don't usually allow anyone into my room. *Some* privacy is essential in a place like this, you know.
CALDER:	I agree. Only what I have to say to you is *so* private that I think—if you don't mind—
MR APPLETON:	Oh—well. There's only one chair.
CALDER:	The bed will do nicely.

(<u>BED SPRINGS</u>)

CALDER:	I'll come straight to the point.

On a night in June 1944 the Carlyon Hotel in South Kensington was hit, by what must have been one of the first doodlebugs of the war. One of the badly mutilated bodies was identified, by papers in his pocket, as Charles Cranston, late Head Cashier of the Ovaz Group, who had vanished a month before, leaving a deficit behind him of around ten thousand pounds in cash. The Police had their hands full of other matters—it was just before D-Day and they were glad to regard the case as closed. The Ovaz management were not so happy. Because none of the missing money was ever found, it was assumed that Cranston had stashed it away somewhere and the secret had died with him. (Slight pause)

MR APPLETON: (In a strangled voice) Is that all?

CALDER: By no means. Here's where the story becomes really interesting. One of the other guests registered at the hotel was a Mr Appleton, a bachelor, without any close connections.

129

He'd been excused military service because of a tubercular history, and had spent the war doing various clerical jobs. No doubt he would carry all his identification documents with him—most of us did in war time.

MR APPLETON: No doubt.

CALDER: Now this Mr Appleton happened to be very much the same general size and shape as the defaulting Cranston. So when Cranston—and I give him credit for it—forced his way into the next door bedroom, after the bomb fell, to see if he could help, and found his neighbour not only dead but mutilated beyond possibility of recognition—it was a matter of minutes, to exchange identity documents, and accept the new personality handed to him by benevolent chance. (<u>Slower</u>) Am I right so far, Mr Appleton—Cranston?

MR APPLETON: How did you find out?

CALDER: Don't let's worry about that. Am I right?

MR APPLETON: In all except one thing. It wasn't pure chance. I'd already

130

been struck by Appleton's resemblance to me. From talking to him, I knew that he had very few connections. I had meant to offer him money— quite a lot of money if he would exchange personalities. Then fate did it for me.

CALDER: I see.

MR APPLETON: What are you going to do? You have a warrant, I imagine?

CALDER: I'm not a policeman, Mr Appleton.

MR APPLETON: You're—

CALDER: Nor have I any particular tenderness for the Ovaz Group, who were making optical instruments for the Air Force—and no doubt had a very profitable war.

MR APPLETON: Do the Police know?

CALDER: At the moment they don't. But I'm afraid that they will—in about twenty-four hours at the latest. However, you are a man of resource. You've slipped them once already. You have your money with you. There are still quite a few countries which have no extradition treaties with us. But I should give you one word of advice.

131

Wherever you land up next, *if* you decide to keep your moveable wealth under your bed, you should remember that there are windows, and that windows are sometimes overlooked from roof-tops. Good-bye, Mr Appleton. And the best of luck.

(<u>FADE OUT</u>:-)

(<u>FADE IN ON</u>:-)

FORTESCUE: Incredible, Behrens. Really quite incredible. Do you imagine that in *all* preparatory schools *all* the staff have skeletons in their cupboards?

BEHRENS: Oh, I shouldn't think so, Sir. I fancy that St Ethelburga's is rather above average in that respect.

FORTESCUE : I hope so. Of our three possibles, the Physical Training Instructor turns out to be a deserter from the armed forces, the Assistant Headmaster to be an embezzler on the run, and the Music Master, by a process of elimination, must be a Nazi war criminal.

132

BEHRENS:	Always supposing that our original supposition was correct.
FORTESCUE:	There has been corroboration. The Police have been monitoring telephone calls to the neo-Nazi group. They have received no fewer than six from Seahampton in the last three months.
BEHRENS:	From Seahampton? Not from St Ethelburga's?
FORTESCUE:	Not from the school itself, naturally. They were made from a public telephone box in the town. But some further facts have also come to light about Mr Abigail. It would appear that his L.R.C.M. is imaginary. The Royal College have no record of him. Moreover, when he first went to Seahampton in 1946 and started looking for teaching jobs, he had to offer some sort of testimonials. We have managed to get hold of one and check it. I fear that it, like his L.R.C.M., is fictitious.
BEHRENS:	Mmm. Fascinating. What do you want me to do about it?
FORTESCUE:	I suggest that you pass the

information immediately to Calder, and let him take the appopriate steps.

(FADE OUT:-)

(FADE IN ON:-)

DAVID RAWNSLEY: Come on, Rasselas. Walk's over.

MICHAEL MELDRUM: No time. Back you come.

DAVID RAWNSLEY: Hullo, Sir. He seems to enjoy his walks so much he doesn't want to get back. What's he saying?

CALDER: He's saying, how'd you like to live in a cricket pavilion? Draughty place. Stinks of linseed oil.

MICHAEL MELDRUM: I say, is it true about Apples?

CALDER: (Cautiously) Is what true?

DAVID RAWNSLEY: He's run off.

MICHAEL MELDRUM: There was a police car up here this morning whilst we were in first period.

DAVID RAWNSLEY: Now that you've unmasked the villain, I suppose you'll be off, and we'll get some other lunatic like Kellaway. Pity.

MICHAEL MELDRUM: We shall miss you.

CALDER: Be honest. What you mean is you'll miss the dog. Well, I'm not going just yet. I've one piece of work to finish.

(<u>FADE OUT</u>:-)

(<u>FADE IN ON</u>:-)
(<u>THE SOUND OF A PIANO BEING PLAYED, WITH CONSIDERABLE EXPERTISE</u>)

(<u>DOOR</u>)

MR ABIGAIL: Ah, Calder! Come in.

CALDER: Sorry to interrupt you, Abigail.

MR ABIGAIL: Not at all. I was just practising.

CALDER: You play very well. So well that I am sure that if you applied, now, to the Royal College of Music, they could not fail to elect you licentiate.

(<u>A BRIEF SILENCE</u>)

MR ABIGAIL: I'm afraid—I don't quite understand—

CALDER: You understand very well. The letters L.R.C.M. after your name are as false as the credentials you presented to various schools around here when you came here in 1946.

135

As false as your name itself. Don't make any rash or sudden move, Dr Fleischmann. You are an old man now, and unfit for violence.

MR ABIGAIL: (<u>Genuinely puzzled</u>) What are you talking about?— Fleischmann—I've never heard the name.

CALDER: No?

MR ABIGAIL: You've stumbled on my secret. God knows how! Are you going to squeeze money out of it too. You may be unlucky. There's not much left to squeeze.

CALDER: I think you'd better do some plain talking—and quickly.

MR ABIGAIL: What's the point of talking, if you know it all?

CALDER: Nevertheless, I'd like to hear it.

MR ABIGAIL: So that you can gloat about it.

CALDER: My motives, Mr Abigal, are unimportant. I want the facts.

MR ABIGAIL: Very well. I joined up in the ranks when war broke out.

CALDER: Regiment?

MR ABIGAIL: The Royal Artillery Depot. Then the 143 Field Regiment B. Battery. I went to North Africa with them. I was 34 when I joined up—a bit old. I'd been in a Bank. And I'd had

	rather a sedentary life. I'm not making excuses—
CALDER:	Shell-shock?
MR ABIGAIL:	That was the polite word for it. They brought me back to England, and I spent the rest of the war in—well—they called it a convalescent home.
CALDER:	Where?
MR ABIGAIL:	At Mersham near Wellington in Shropshire.
CALDER:	Then?
MR ABIGAIL:	When the war ended, they let me out. What could I do? The Bank wouldn't consider me. I was still unfit. I came down here. One day, one of the Headmasters was telling me how difficult it was to get qualified music teachers. I played the piano competently, that was all that mattered. It was a living. (<u>Pause</u>) What's going to become of me now?
CALDER:	Provided those details you have given me check up, and I'm certain they will, because I can see no earthly reason why you should have lied about matters which can be checked so easily—then as far as I am concerned, Mr Abigail, you

137

	may continue to teach music to all the Preparatory Schools in Seahampton.
MR ABIGAIL:	—you mean—?
CALDER:	I said, as far as I was concerned. When we started this conversation you asked, 'Was I going to squeeze money out of you, *too*?' I want to know who else has your secret, and who's been blackmailing you. (<u>Pause</u>)
MR ABIGAIL:	If I told you, you wouldn't believe me.
CALDER:	Try me.

(<u>FADE OUT</u>:-)

(<u>FADE IN ON TELEPHONE BELL AND CLICK AS RECEIVER IS REMOVED</u>)

CALDER:	Calder, here.
FORTESCUE:	Fortescue speaking. I'm telephoning you direct, and on an open line, because I think that speed may be more important than secrecy. Behrens has made the most extraordinary discovery. He managed to extract from our American friends the family

138

name—the original Polish family name of Fleischmann. It was Menarski. It is not a common name, and Behrens is quite positive that there is only one record of a child being born to these people at any relevant period.

CALDER: That's all right, Sir. I know what you're going to say. I found it out for myself an hour ago.

FORTESCUE: Indeed. Then I need say no more. You can deal with it.

CALDER: (<u>Grimly</u>) I'll deal with it.

(<u>FADE OUT</u>:-)

(<u>FADE IN ON</u>:-)

MATRON: And what can I do for you, Mr Calder? If it's medical attention you want, perhaps we had better go down to the surgery.

CALDER: No.

MATRON: I don't usually receive people in my private room.

CALDER: On this occasion it would I think, be wiser. The matters we have to discuss are not really suitable for young ears.

MATRON:	I was not aware that I had anything to discuss with you.
CALDER:	Not one thing. Two. Let us deal with the less important one first. How did you discover that Mr Abigail was not a qualified music teacher?
MATRON:	(In a new voice, which gets progressively harder as the scene develops) So that soppy old fool has been talking, has he. I found out the same way that you probably did. I made an enquiry at the College of Music.
CALDER:	Simple. And how much have you been extracting from him?
MATRON:	That's nothing to do with you. Unless you're after a cut of it.
CALDER:	No. I fancy we might leave him in peace now, Doktor Fleischmann.
MATRON:	So that has been discovered too.
CALDER:	It wasn't very difficult. Once we had your family name of Menarski. The only birth registered under that name was to Jon and Olgar Menarski on the 17th June 1910—a daughter, Maria. Why did you pose as a man when you went

140

to Germany to work as a doctor?

MATRON: Do you imagine they'd have accepted me, if I hadn't. You know what the Fuehrer thought about women—Kinder, Kuche, Kirke.

CALDER: I see. Very ingenious. Then, when you reached England, you simply reverted to your proper sex. Do you know if you hadn't sent money to our fledgling Nazis here I really believe you'd have got away with it. That was stupid, you know.

MATRON: Do you imagine I sent it willingly. One of them had stumbled on the truth.

CALDER: So! Poetic justice! You were blackmailing Abigail—they were blackmailing you.

MATRON: And what makes you think that I can't get away with it, even now? I paid those fools because they had some nuisance value, not because they could prove anything in Court. I am Maria Menarski. I was born in England. I have every right to be here—under any name I wish to use. This German

141

episode—Fleischmann—a fable. Prove it if you can.

CALDER: You misjudge me, Fraulein Doktor. I have no intention of trying to prove the facts to an English Court. I have arranged for a much more efficient, and interested, tribunal.

MATRON: (<u>An edge of fear</u>) What do you mean?

CALDER: In a very short time—a matter of days—you will be kidnapped by one of the Jewish teams who specialise in this work, and will stand trial in Israel for the crimes you have committed against humanity.

(<u>FADE OUT</u>:-)

(<u>FADE IN ON</u>:-)

CALDER: So Maria Menarski stood the suspense for four days. Then she took poison. Cyanide. The traditional way out.

FORTESCUE: A foul end, Calder, for a foul woman. It'll be brought in as suicide while the balance of her mind was disturbed.

CALDER: Actually, it's Mr Pellumpton who's nearly out of his mind.

142

Do you realise that inside one week he's lost an Assistant Head, a Matron and a Judo Instructor.

FORTESCUE: Well, we must look through the files of the Department, and see if we can't help him out, Behrens!

BEHRENS: Oh no, sir! We have undertaken a number of hazardous assignments for the department, but teaching in *that* school seems to me to be beyond the call of duty.

(<u>MUSIC UP AND OUT</u>)

THE GREAT GERMAN SPY HUNT

There are seasons in our lives that are golden. Time itself has gilded and varnished them; the shadows are gone, and the highlights are set for ever. The late summer of 1920 is, with me, such a period.

Every day was golden, starting with a true, autumnal mist, continuing with skies of clear but faded blue, deepening into blood red as the sun set and promised another lovely day to follow.

Since it was my first term at a preparatory school, on the South Coast (I have never known such weather there again; since 1920 a healthful but nipping sea breeze seems to have been blowing through my memory of it); since, as I say, it was my first term at boarding school, and I was barely eight years old, it would not, perhaps, be expected to be a time of joyful memories. I believe that all boarding schools now are so enlightened and well-conducted that boys are happy the whole term through, deploring the holidays as an unnecessary interruption. I can only say that it was not so then, or not in most schools. I think this particular school was run by exceptional people and was ahead of its time, for I can never remember being really unhappy there. But that autumn remains a special memory.

I slept in a dormitory called Nelson; others were named Wellington and Clive and Havelock after the brutal and successful warriors of our Imperial past. I feel no doubt that this, too, is changed for the better now. All the same, I shall remove my boy if anyone attempts to put him in a dormitory called Summerskill.

The background of our lives at that time was the 1914–18 war—or, as we then called it, the Great War. Veterans in the school could remember the lean winters of '16, '17 and '18 when commons were short and fuel was scarce, and warmth was only maintained in class by non-stop rowdyism, facilitated by the fact that most of the teachers were women.

The school had had, in the past few years, joint headmasters. On reflection I think that the arrangement they came to was a remarkably sensible one. Being accustomed, as experienced pedagogues, to sharing duties on a rota basis, they had decided to share the war. Estimating its probable duration as four years (an estimate which, in 1914, was shared by Lord Kitchener, but few other people) one of them joined the Army from 1914 to 1916, and was then relieved by the other, who fought on until 1918.

At the time I arrived it was the second headmaster, affectionately known to his pupils as Buggins—and still, I am glad to say, alive—who had taken over the school. His second in command, Tich, is also still flourishing. There must be something preservative about those fresh, South Coast breezes.

However, it is the aftermath of the war that I was particularly recalling. On the downs which rise between the School and the sea there still stood vast hutted encampments in which the citizen soldiers had lived, and trained, before crossing to a France which was visible, on clear days, from the top of the Seven Sisters.

There were white patches still on the downs where Zeppelins had jettisoned their bombs, and there were watchman's huts, lonely little sentry posts, the barbed wire round them now rusty and ineffective, on most of the prominent and seaward-looking headland.

*   *   *

I have come to the conclusion that, in our minds at least, the war was still going on. Boys are naturally conservative. I conclude this from my memories of the great German spy hunt. Before describing this I must introduce Christopher, who had the bed next to mine. Christopher and I were in alliance, and it was natural that, as soon as it occurred to him that there were German spies in the school, he should have told me about it.

146

The first, or master spy, was the mathematics master. In case he may still, too, be living I shall withhold his name and refer to him as X. X when one came to think of it, was an obvious choice. He had smooth black, shiny hair, drove a powerful car (it made so much noise that it must have been powerful) and he was an expert in photography; all attributes of the professional spy. He first gave himself away by taking a pair of binoculars on a walk with him and studying, through them, one of the deserted sentry huts. Clearly an assignation was being arranged at the hut—a natural meeting place for spies, being conspicuous and difficult to get at. But an assignation meant a fellow spy. Close vigilance should enable us to discover his identity.

The unmasking of the second spy was accomplished soon afterwards. He was a young visiting master, who masqueraded under the name of Mr Thompson, and taught drawing. This, in itself, was suggestive, as was the fact that he came to school on a motor bicycle with a side car. But definite proof was not forthcoming for some time. As far as we could see X never spoke to Mr Thompson, nor Mr Thompson to X. This was suspicious.

A quick examination of the side car revealed a torch and a pair of goloshes. But it was not to be expected that an experienced spy would leave anything that mattered in his sidecar. It was the briefcase, which he carried with him, that contained the incriminating evidence. Of that we were sure. But how to get at it? It would have been possible, in theory, to knock him out in the dark passage leading from the changing room but from this, somehow, we shrank. In the end, fate played into our hands. He was on his way to the classroom to give a drawing lesson, when the headmaster came out of his study and summoned him. Mr Thompson placed the briefcase on a locker, and went in. I was watching from the class room door, and was out like a flash. One glance inside the briefcase was enough. Nestling among the drawing blocks, the spare pencils and rubbers was—a German phrase book!

*　　*　　*

I sought out Christopher in triumph and trepidation, which he promptly managed to increase. The number of our enemies was not two. Two adult and vindictive enemy agents would have been bad enough. Now it was three, and the latest was in some ways the worst.

By a process of close observation, Christopher had discovered that the assistant Matron—her name I seem to remember was Miss Helmore—was really a man. And if a man, clearly a German.

Whilst I, imagining myself daring, had been investigating the drawing master's briefcase, Christopher had performed a feat beside which mine paled into insignificance. He had penetrated to the assistant Matron's bedroom and there had found, insolently displayed on the top of a chest of drawers, a pair of dark glasses and a bottle of hair dye. Nor was this all. Confident that he was on the right track, and that the police, if not the School authorities, would back him up if he was discovered, he had actually opened one of the drawers. And there the full truth had been revealed, for nestling among garments of an apparently female nature, was a safety razor.

'And when you look closely,' said Christopher, 'you can see that she—he, I mean—wears a wig.'

At bed time that evening we both looked closely. There was no doubt about it. The assistant Matron looked closely at us in return, and remarked that we looked pale. Was there anything wrong with us?

There seemed to be a sinister undertone to her question, and when she insisted on us having a spoonful of Parishes Food we managed, by distracting her attention, to tip it into a flower vase. She wasn't going to silence us that easily.

It was clear, however, that something had to be done. We consulted Derek, who was nine years old and a fearless and militant character, as he subsequently proved in the war against Hitler. Although he was deeply busied in his own affairs—he had become an atheist and was engaged in a campaign to wreck the Sunday evening service by coaching rival factions, one of whom was to say the General Confession very fast, and the other very slowly—as soon as he realized the gravity of the situation he devoted himself wholeheartedly to our problems.

In the end he came to the conclusion that the whole matter must be reported to the headmaster. Moreover, to our relief, he undertook to do so himself at the first suitable opportunity.

After lunch was the occasion for all official pronouncements, pleasant and unpleasant, and it was on the following day that the headmaster, after dealing with a small matter of window-breaking, declared 'You will all be sorry to hear that neither Mr Thompson nor Miss Helmore will be with us next term'. Christopher and I looked round at Derek, who was staring impassively in front of him. 'For a pleasant reason, however' went on the headmaster, 'as they have become engaged to be married. A voluntary collection will be started for a wedding present from the boys. I shall arrange for sixpence to be deducted from your pocket money next week'.

X left shortly afterwards, as well. It was

rumoured that he was taking up a post abroad.

I said at the beginning that I could never remember such a summer as 1920. I had forgotten. There was another. It was June, of 1940, and day by day the skies were of deep blue, without cloud but criss-crossed by the white vapour trails of the Spitfires, some of them, I am sure, flown by boys who had been at school with me twenty years earlier, as they jinked and played with the enemy in the corridors of the upper air. Having a weekend's leave and nothing to do with it, I had wandered down to the South Coast. And at the end of the school drive I found Tich in person. He was alone, for he had just sent all the staff and boys home, as a first move towards evacuating the school to Cornwall.

Suddenly there appeared a small fleet of cars. In the front one, smoking a cigar but not, at that period, making the V-sign, was the Prime Minister. We were unsurprised to see him. He was much on the South Coast in those weeks, between Dover and Portsmouth. What was odd, however, was that his cortege appeared to be drawing to the side, to allow passage to another, coming in the opposite direction. Surely the Prime Minister should have right of way? Then we saw that it was the King, also on a tour of the defences. The convoys stopped. Salutes and greetings were exchanged. It was a historic moment. But my mind was not entirely in the present. Suddenly, in a flash, I saw it all. It was for just such a moment that the German Intelligence had made their plans. Unerringly they had deduced the vital spot. Only they had planted their agents too soon. Ruthless, painstaking, but premature by twenty years.

THE KILLING OF KARL CARVER

Detective Superintendent Samkin sighed with relief when he reached Dr Crooke's front door. This was no ordinary rainstorm. It was a cloud burst. A North London special. Water had seeped inside the turned up collar of his raincoat and splashed up over his shoes.

The front door was on the latch. A familiar voice from the room at the back roared out: 'If it's you, Terence, come right in. If it's anyone else, get lost.' Samkin grinned and pushed open the door. Dr Hamar Crooke had stockinged feet stretched out to a roaring fire of logs. He climbed out of his chair as Samkin came in.

'Man, you're soaking. Let me have that coat. Thank God I wasn't persuaded to take a modern flat. Fancy sitting in front of a radiator on a night like this! Take off your shoes. I expect your socks are wet too. A straight malt whisky is my prescription.'

The Superintendent would have passed unnoticed in a crowd. Dr Crooke would almost certainly have been recognised. The Home Office pathologist had featured in so many murder cases that his shock of grey hair and his heavy pince-nez glasses, insecurely fixed on a bulb of a nose, had become household features.

He and the Superintendent were old friends, old hunters in the forests of crime; but their conversation that evening was not about crime and criminals. As Samkin's grey woollen socks steamed in the heat of the fire they talked about Protone Seven.

'It's had such a hell of a build-up,' said Samkin, 'that if it doesn't do everything the advertisements claim, people will be clamouring for their money back.'

'Of course it will do what it claims,' said Crooke.

The Superintendent was looking at the evening newspaper which carried a full-page advertisement. He said: 'Can any concoction really relieve tension, alleviate anxiety, allow you to sleep through the night and awake refreshed and invigorated?'

'Why not? Tension and insomnia are mental states. If you believe that what you are taking will cure them, they will be cured.'

'Faith healing?'

'If you like.'

'The formula,' Samkin read, 'is known only to the directors of Carver Pharmaceutical Enterprises.'

'And consists, I would guess, of a small quantity of one of the more common sedatives, a dash of commercial alcohol and aqua pura. The stuff we're drinking is older and sounder medicine. A refill?'

As he moved to the side-board the

telephone rang. Crooke said, 'I won't answer it.'

'You'd better,' said Samkin. 'I have to let our people know where I can be found. It may be for me.'

Dr Crooke picked up the telephone. 'It is for you. Karl Carver has been shot. They want you at once.'

'If they want me,' said Samkin, 'they'll certainly want you. We'll go in your car.'

As the car bucketed down-hill with its wipers working overtime, Samkin said: 'Carver was quite a character. Came here from Hungary after the war. His real name was Karva. Karl Karva. He had a chemical business in his own country, but he landed here with nothing but his brains and business flair. He built up C.P.E. to what it is now. It was his family, his life and his religion. Did you ever meet him?'

'I remember going to one of his garden parties; I guessed he must be stinking rich if he owned two acres of walled garden in North London. There was a bishop there and an actress. This is the place, isn't it?'

The young Detective Inspector in charge seemed relieved at the appearance of reinforcements.

'All right, Wilmot,' said Samkin. 'I'll take over. You're treating it as murder?'

'Carver was shot, in his study, upstairs. And the gun's missing.'

155

'I'll take Doctor Crooke up. As soon as he's finished, the photographers and finger-print people can get started. Keep everyone downstairs for the moment.'

The door at the head of the stairs was ajar. Samkin nudged it further open and they went through.

Karl Carver was seated in a high chair behind a large plain desk which was covered with files and papers neatly stacked. There were two telephones on the desk, a tape-recorder and a battery-operated calculator. The bullet had hit him in the middle of the forehead and had thrown him back into the chair.

'A small clean entry wound,' said Crooke. 'I'd guess the killer wasn't more than a few feet away when he fired. Probably just this side of the desk.'

'Would you let an unknown walk up to you, and not even try to get up, or push your chair back?'

'It raises an assumption that he knew the killer,' agreed Crooke.

'How long has he been dead?'

'That shouldn't be difficult to fix accurately. A warm room, even temperature, no draughts.' He was taking thermometers and other apparatus out of the bag he had brought with him. Samkin left him to it. There was much to do.

He found three people in the drawing room.

Karl Carver's daughter, Penelope, was sitting on the sofa: not a pretty girl, but attractive in the hard modern idiom. The pale young man beside her would be Simon Blewitt, Carver's secretary. In the chair by the fireplace, as though disassociating herself by this remove from the other two, sat the thick, grey-haired Miss Mardyke, who had run the house since the death of Carver's wife, six years before. 'A strong-minded woman,' said Wilmot. 'I don't think the other two like her much. They're engaged, by the way.'

Samkin introduced himself and said, 'What can you tell me about this?'

Miss Mardyke said, in her deep voice: 'I found Mr Carver in his room when I went up. I telephoned the Police Station at once.'

'Did you use the telephone in the hall or the one on his desk?'

Miss Mardyke looked surprised, and said: 'The one on his desk, of course. I didn't want to waste time.'

'Did you have any particular reason for going up?'

'No. But since he'd been alone for nearly two hours I thought I'd better see if he wanted anything.'

There was a slight movement from the sofa. 'They know about that,' thought Samkin. 'And they don't like it.'

'Earlier in the evening I'd had a telephone call. A man who said he was speaking from

157

Walthamstow Hospital. Where one of my sisters works. She's Senior Theatre Sister. He said she'd collapsed on duty, could I come at once.'

'And when you got there?'

'It seemed there was nothing wrong at all. In fact, she was in the theatre taking part in a rather complicated operation.'

'Why do you suppose anyone would do a thing like that to you?'

Miss Mardyke glanced at the pair on the sofa and seemed, at the last moment, to alter what she had been going to say.

I can only assume that it was a pointless and rather cruel trick.'

'And you got back—?'

'At the same time as these two.'

'What time was that?'

The three looked at each other. In the end it was Miss Mardyke who said, 'I wasn't looking at clocks. It would have been about 8.30.'

Penelope said: 'That would be about right. We all came in together. Miss Mardyke told us about her telephone call. I think I suggested she went up. Daddy never liked being left alone for too long.'

Samkin thought: 'She's taking it all very calmly.' Simon Blewitt seemed more upset than she was. He said, in a squeaky, disjointed voice: 'That's not quite true, you know.'

'What's not true?'

'That we all arrived together. Miss Mardyke

158

was at the door when we came up the steps.'

Miss Mardyke said, impassively: 'I got here just ahead of you. As I was closing the door I heard you at the gate and opened it again for you.'

Samkin looked at the secretary and said, drawing his words out deliberately: 'I'm sure you all appreciate the gravity of the situation. If any of you know anything that might help . . .'

There was a moment of silence, and then Simon said: 'I've got to speak to you alone, Superintendent.'

'If this report is right,' said the Assistant Commissioner, 'any woman who took Protone Seven at any stage of pregnancy would be liable to produce a blind child.' He turned to the last page. 'Dated, I see, two days ago and signed by Dr Bacarach and Dr Melluish. Do you know them?'

'Everyone knows them,' said Dr Crooke. 'Lionel Bacarach has been working in this field for 40 years. His mental processes may be a little stiff, but his experience is unrivalled. Andrew Melluish was my first and one of my most efficient assistants. Incidentally, he's not only a biologist, he's an excellent mechanic. He's the only doctor I've ever known who could take an X-ray machine to pieces and put it together again. If those two names are on the report, you can take it as gospel.'

'Could Carver have suppressed it? Surely the doctors would have insisted on publication.'

'I'm not sure,' said Crooke. 'Carver was a fanatic. And the report was confidential. They'd been commissioned by the company to make it. A very difficult question of professional ethics.'

'Ethics be blowed,' said Samkin hotly. 'Surely . . .'

The Assistant Commissioner said smoothly: 'Apart from the two doctors, who knew about this report?'

'Carver's deputy at C.P.E., Sir Edward Galloway, knew that the report had been asked for. He may have guessed what was in it. He might also have suspected that Carver might suppress it.'

'How did the secretary find out about it?'

'He had the spare keys of the safe. His version is that he was looking for something else, saw the report, and read it out of curiosity. Just snooping, I fancy.'

'Five people, then,' said the Assistant Commissioner.

'Plus anyone they may have told,' said Samkin. 'Blewitt was engaged to Carver's daughter and they were out together that evening.'

'Yes, I think we must include her. A lot is going to turn on times.'

'Fortunately,' said Crooke, 'I can give you

160

quite narrow limits. A body loses heat at the rate of one degree an hour after death. Here there were several helpful factors. The speed with which we were called in. The level temperature of a centrally heated room. The fact that Carver, possibly because he recognised the intruder, wasn't mentally or physically disturbed. A shock, or violent action immediately before death can raise the temperature artificially.

'Anyone who can demonstrate conclusively that they were elsewhere at eight o'clock is out of the reckoning.'

'What time was the body found?'

Samkin said: 'The three parties concerned were curiously vague. In the end they settled for 8.30. Actually, it must have been earlier. Wilmot logged the telephone call at 8.25. He rang me up at once and we got there just before nine.'

The Assistant Commissioner said: 'It's theoretically possible that this killing was done by an outsider; that it was a coincidence and unconnected with this report. Every instinct I've got tells me that's nonsense. This was a deliberate murder, timed to the minute, with a carefully arranged alibi. What we must have is every available detail of what each of those six people was doing between, shall we say, to be safe, 7.30 and 8.30.'

'I've told you exactly what I did,' said Miss Mardyke. 'I left at 6.45 p.m. and took a

Bakerloo train to Oxford Circus, changed on to the Victoria Line for Walthamstow Central. The journey takes 35 minutes. Then it's a 10-minute walk to the hospital. I suppose I was a quarter of an hour talking to the Matron. As soon as she had established that the call was a hoax I came back! I got back at 8.30.'

'Last time I asked you,' said Samkin, 'you didn't seem entirely clear about when you got back.'

'I have spoken to Miss Carver and Mr Blewitt. They are now both certain they got back at 8.30. Since I arrived with them, I must have got back at the same time.'

'You checked the hospital,' said the Assistant Commissioner.

'Certainly. The matron remembers Sister Mardyke's sister turning up at about half past seven with this story of a telephone call. When it was confirmed that Sister Mardyke was in perfectly good health, they chatted for a bit and Miss Mardyke left.'

'Did Miss Mardyke know about this report?'

'She could have done. When Simon Blewitt had read it, he put it back in the safe, but forgot to lock it.'

'Even if she had read it, would she have understood it?'

'I think so. They're an intelligent family. One, as you know, is a senior Theatre Sister. Another is a vet. They're none of them married.'

162

'That demonstrates their intelligence,' said the Assistant Commissioner, who was a bachelor.

'I gather,' said Samkin, 'that you and Miss Carver went out together that evening.'

'That's right,' said Simon Blewitt. 'And we're engaged to be married, so I don't suppose you'll believe a word I say.'

'I wouldn't go as far as that,' said Samkin. 'Just tell me what you did.'

'We went to Trafalgar Square. We'd booked a table at Boulestins for 6.30. We both like eating early. When we got out we looked in at the News Theatre, in the Strand.'

'What did you see?'

'Those programmes are all pretty much alike. Two or three cartoons and a newsreel, I think.'

'Where did you sit?'

'Good heavens,' said Simon, 'how should I know? They're as black as pitch. The girl shines a torch on a seat and you sit down.'

'How long did it take to get home?'

'The same time as it took us to get out, I imagine.'

'I gather,' said Samkin, 'that you and Mr Blewitt went out together that evening.'

'Correct,' said Penelope crisply.

'What did you do?'

'We caught a Bakerloo Line train at St John's Wood and got out at Trafalgar Square. The journey, at that time of day, takes 12 minutes. We arrived at 6.20 and walked to Boulestins Restaurant. We were almost the only people there at that hour and the service was quick. We were out before 7.30 and we put in threequarters of an hour at the News Theatre.'

'What did you see?'

'We didn't have time for the whole programme. We saw three Walt Disney cartoons, a travelogue about the Rocky Mountains and a newsreel.'

'Where did you sit?'

'We were lucky to get a seat. We found one in the back row.'

'They must have remembered them at Boulestins,' said the Assistant Commissioner.

'They certainly did,' said Samkin. 'And they confirm that they were clear before 7.30. No luck at the News Theatre. It's the most crowded time, lots of young couples going in and out. So much for the three insiders. Now for the outsiders.'

'There's one point I find puzzling about the outsiders,' said the Assistant Commissioner. 'One of them could have got rid of Miss Mardyke by telephoning. But how would he have known that the secretary and daughter were out?'

'No difficulty,' said Samkin. 'He'd ring up again. If anyone else was in the house, they'd answer from the hall. If Carver was alone, he'd take the call in his study and say that everyone else was out.'

'How would an outsider get in?'

'A back kitchen window had been forced.'

'That doesn't prove that it was an outsider,' said the Assistant Commissioner. 'It could be a bluff.'

'I'm far from clear why you're asking,' said Dr Bacarach. 'But in fact I was playing bridge at my club. The other three were Brigadier Alnott, my stockbroker Ralph Robey and Sir Eric Pettifer.'

'I take it you've checked?' the Assistant Commissioner asked.

'Certainly. The only curious thing was that none of them seemed able to remember who won.'

'I thought that was the one thing bridge players always remembered,' said the Assistant Commissioner.

'They let me use this flat in the hospital,' said Dr Melluish. 'It's handy during the week when I'm working here at St Luke's. I only wish they'd built the walls a bit thicker. I can hear my neighbour Dr Bland hammering out a thesis on his typewriter. I reciprocate by keeping my wireless on,' he told Samkin.

'You're fond of classical music?'

'All sorts. If you're asking about that night . . .' he fished out a copy of *Radio Times*. '. . .I was listening to *Sports Report* at 6.45, followed by a record programme on Radio One. I switched over at 7.45 to catch the Brahms

Second, played by the Northern Symphony Orchestra. I finished listening at 8.30 and went downstairs to have dinner.'

'And you never left your room or went out during that time?'

'Certainly not. It was raining cats and dogs.'

'The only time he must have been in his room is 7.45,' said the Assistant Commissioner.

'That's right,' said Samkin. 'Dr Bland heard him switch over.'

'How long would it take him to get from St Luke's to Carver's flat by car at that time of night?'

'Roughly half an hour.'

'I think that lets him out,' said the Assistant Commissioner.

'Where was I that night?' said Sir Edward Galloway. 'I was at my club. I went there from the office. I had a drink and hung around hoping the rain would ease off. I left about 7.15 and took a taxi back to my flat in Knightsbridge.'

'Did the porter call it for you?' said Samkin.

'No. I found one in the street.'

'How did you fix the time you left?'

'I telephoned my wife. I happened to mention the time. She'll remember.'

'And she did,' said Samkin later. 'She was vague about everything else, but she did remember her husband saying it was 7.15. She hadn't got a watch or clock to check it by, but she thought it must have been about right. He got back 20 minutes after he telephoned.'

'We must have missed something,' said the Assistant Commissioner. 'Let's look at all of it again.'

*   *   *

To help readers come to a conclusion, Michael Gilbert gave them the following advice. 'It is of course impossible, after so brief a statement, to be mathematically or legally certain who committed the murder; but if the reader plays close attention to the personalities of the candidates and the plausibility of their alibis, and considers the realities of the matter, he should be able to see that one of the candidates is quite outstandingly probable as the murderer.' Who do you think was guilty?

Solution

The solution was printed in the TV Times for 26 June 1976: 'Dr Hamar Crooke, the pathologist, dunnit.' No further information was given.

CLOSE CONTACT

When I left Blundell's, I got a job as assistant master in a preparatory school in a Cathedral Close. We were a job lot. The staff I mean. The boys were normal enough, except that some of them had voices, and sang in the Cathedral choir. But the staff was a team of amateurs headed by one professional.

There were four assistant masters. I was the youngest at 18; the oldest wasn't more than 21, and between us we had about as much knowledge of teaching as we had of life. They are both things you have to pick up and we were strictly beginners.

'S', the headmaster, was a different proposition. All I will say about him across the years is that he was an old-fashioned disciplinarian.

I remember that he used to read us extracts from a book, evidently written by an older and sterner disciplinarian than himself. It was called *Quis Custodiet* and it dealt with the sins and shortcomings of assistant masters.

One of the things 'S' was very keen on was assistant masters getting a full night's rest. The author of *Quis Custodiet* was keen on this too.

No young man, he wrote, could stay up to all hours drinking and dancing and indulging in other such excesses, and be fit to take early Latin Grammar.

There was a certain amount of sense in this although the excuses to be found in this particular Cathedral city were hardly serious enough to worry about.

However, some time in my second term at the school, I made the acquaintance of a hospitable doctor and his wife—they had a son at the school—and they invited me round once or twice for an evening of bridge.

In case you don't play this game, I should explain that it is played by four people with cards, and has one peculiarity. It always goes on longer than you think it is going to. You may start a so-called 'final rubber' with the best of intentions at ten o'clock, and find midnight chiming before you've even got to game-all.

On the first two occasions, by luck and determination, I got back to the Close as 11 was striking.

This was important. Because at 11 sharp the great medieval gates shut with a clang, and you only got inside by ringing the bell and summoning the underporter, a surly character who would be almost bound to report you to your headmaster.

On the third occasion, 11 o'clock slid past almost unnoticed. And, with a feeling that I might as well be hanged for a sheep as a lamb, I let it slide.

It was half-past one when I left, but I was not without a plan. It had long occurred to me that it would be useful to have a private way in, and I imagined that I knew of one.

The walls of this particular Close are battlemented and lofty, but at the southern end I had observed that a much lower garden wall had been built.

It seemed to me that from the top of this wall, the bottom of one of the battlemented embrasures should be within reach. The drop on the other side would be manageable. And the fact that I should then find myself in the garden of the Bishop's palace did not unduly disturb me, since this was only separated from the rest of the Close by a fence and hedge.

It was bright moonlight, which, on the whole, was a help, as with beating heart, I hoisted myself on to the garden wall. The embrasure was within easy reach.

I put my fingers on the ledge, and at this precise moment a pair of hands appeared on the other side followed, a moment later, by a face.

It was difficult to say which of us was more startled, but my opposite number being, as I guess, an old soldier, recovered first. 'What are you up to?' he said. 'Come to that,' I said, 'what are you?'

He was evidently standing on some sort of ledge inside the wall—no doubt the very ledge from which his predecessors had poured down arrows and other missiles on their attackers. He had with him a suitcase, which he now lifted up, and placed on the ledge. He must have decided that I was harmless.

'Matter of fact,' he said, 'I've just been helping myself to old Rowley's silver. He's got plenty to go on with. He won't miss this little lot.'

Canon Rowley, a rich and miserly bachelor, was one of the least popular of the Close's inhabitants. Only a week before he had reported me to the headmaster for allowing the boys to straggle on a walk. And anyway like everyone else at 18, I was a practical communist.

'Serve him right,' I said. 'If I move over, do you think you could squeeze past?'

I held the case for him while he wriggled through—it struck me as remarkably light— and a minute later he was walking away down the street, whistling. Ten minutes later I was in bed.

Next morning I felt less easy. That is one of the troubles about next morning. I began to reflect that there were many other houses my burglar might have robbed. The suitcase had certainly not felt like old silver. Suppose he had visited Mrs Parkes and abstracted the slender savings which, as everyone knew, she kept behind the lavatory cistern; or stolen from poor Dean Bartram, who was so unworldly that he was probably uninsured; or,

171

worst of all, had combined sacrilege with his other offences, and filched the original Canaletto from the Chapter house.

For days I was jumpy. I suffered acute trepidation when someone spoke in my hearing of Mrs Kiffen's 'sad loss'; to be reassured when I understood that it was only her 90-year-old mother that was being referred to. In the end, I forgot the incident almost entirely.

It was more than ten years later that I met my midnight acquaintance again, and I recognised him instantly.

Bombardier X came into my troop, with a squad of reservists, just before we went overseas in 1942. I was fairly confident that he had not recognised me. I had changed a great deal more in every way, in the last decade, than X had.

I looked up his record sheet, which showed him (sure enough) at a station near my school in the early '30s. It also showed his conduct as 'Exemplary' and I was in two minds as to whether to recall to him our previous encounter.

In the end, after six months' campaigning—by which time I knew X a lot better—I did broach the topic.

'Of course it was me, sir,' said X, without batting an eyelid. 'And what's more I recognised you as soon as I saw you again.'

He lied; but I let it pass.

'Why was no theft ever reported?' I asked.

'Theft?' said X indignantly. 'I never took anything. Oh, Old Rowley's silver. I said that because I knew you wouldn't fuss about a thing like that. If you'd known I was after one of the maids at the palace—a nice girl, but a pushover for a soldier—you might have got a bit shirty. Nowadays, of course, it'd be the other way round. I'd tell you about the girl, because you wouldn't mind that, but you might be a bit dodgy about burglary.'

I remember feeling indignant at the time. Thinking it over, I have an awful feeling X may have been right.

THE FIRE-RAISERS

'Her name,' said Tara Fearne, 'is Alison Blakely. I have known her for a long time. Six, seven years maybe. I was at school with her younger sister, Jenny. Alison used to come down and take us both out and stand us scrumptious teas. Alison French, as she was then, before she married Colin. I had an hour with them both yesterday. They're in real trouble, dad. They need help, and need it badly.'

Francis Fearne, the senior partner of Fearne and Bracknell solicitors, grunted with a marked lack of enthusiasm.

'I haven't forgotten the last young lady you brought along who needed help badly.'

His daughter grinned. 'Toni Beauchamp. Yes. She was rather a handful.'

'She took up hours of my time, when I was extremely busy. Ignored my advice, and departed without paying the very modest bill that I presented to her.'

'Oh, Alison's quite different. She's a respectable married woman. And, anyway, it's not Alison who's in trouble. It's her husband, Colin. I had an hour with them yesterday.'

'If half of what I've been reading about them in the papers is true, they're certainly in trouble. Suspected arson and fraud, isn't it?'

'The papers,' said Tara scornfully. 'They always pick out the bad bits.'

'Naturally. The bad bits are what their readers enjoy. No one wants to read about a virtuous young man, who saves his money and is faithful to his wife.' Before Tara could accuse him, as she was about to do, of being a prejudiced old frump, he added, 'Very well. Tell me the whole story. All that I know personally about Colin Blakely—apart from what I've read in the papers—stands to his credit. I bought the best squash racquet I ever had from his shop.'

'It was a lovely shop. Full of everything to do with every game you've ever thought of.'

'Full of everything that could induce you to take more exercise than was good for you. Thus ensuring the early death from heart failure of any middle aged man who fancied that he was young again. Sorry. Ignore that last bit. Just the voice of envy speaking. You said it *was* a lovely shop. Do I gather that it's all gone now?'

'No. The building itself is all right. The fire was brought under control pretty quickly, which was lucky, as the Blakelys lived in a flat over the shop. What was totally destroyed was the things in the shop.'

'All those lovely tennis and squash racquets,' said Fearne sadly. 'It must have broken Blakely's heart to see them go up in flames.'

'Exactly,' said Tara. 'And that's what makes

nonsense of the supposition that he started the fire himself. He couldn't have done it. It's impossible.'

'Improbable. Not impossible.'

'No,' said Tara firmly. 'Impossible. He could no more have set fire to those lovely things than he could have burned his own children.'

'Very well,' said Fearne. 'I'll take your word for it. But I'll have to consult the others.'

By which he meant his partners. Bob Bracknell and Bob's son, Hugo. Fearne and Bracknell had, at that time, quite enough clients to keep them busy. Taking on a new client required the vote of all four partners, and the tacit approval, if not the actual vote, of their managing clerk, Mr Piggin.

'I've talked to Piggy,' said Tara. 'He's all for it. Hugo wasn't enthusiastic, but he won't say no.' 'And what about Bob?'

Robert Bracknell, number two in the partnership, was a man of decided views.

'I'd hoped you'd tackle him,' said Tara. 'He'll listen to you.'

'He'll listen. Doesn't mean he'll agree. And I shan't be arguing all that strongly. Just bear in mind that we're not criminal lawyers. We make most of our money from family business. Respectable family business.'

'When I became a partner,' said Tara, 'you told me that we would work for anyone who needed our help and was willing and able to pay our fees.'

'Good Lord,' said Fearne. 'Did I say that?'

'You certainly did. And I've never forgotten it.'

'You say you had an hour with Colin and Alison yesterday. I imagine you made an attendance note.'

'Of course,' said Tara. She produced two pages of typescript.

'I'll need copies for my partners.'

'Three copies here.' She added them to the sheets on the table. 'I've done one for Piggy as well.'

His junior partner was certainly putting her back into the matter, thought Fearne, as he started to read. The note opened with a verbatim account of what Colin Blakely had told Tara.

'It began with a telephone call at about 1.50 p.m. on Thursday last, October 10th. I'd shut the shop, as I usually did between 1 o'clock and 2 o'clock, and I was upstairs, when the telephone rang, just finishing my lunch. I'd had to get it for myself, as my wife was away for the day, visiting her mother, who was in hospital.'

(These things always seemed to start with a telephone call, thought Fearne. He remembered the Banting affair, which he'd been concerned with, and the classic Wallace case, in which he had taken no part, but about which he had read more than once. Was it not a mysterious telephone call that had set

William Herbert Wallace off on a fruitless search for the non-existent Qualtrough?)

'The caller wasn't known to me—a Mr Robinson—but he knew of my interest in sports gear. He told me that he had managed to get hold of a consignment of trainers—shoes that are in constant demand by the young and are correspondingly in short supply. He was offering me the whole lot, with a suitable mark-up for himself. The overall price was certainly tempting. I said I'd be right along, and asked where he was speaking from. How'd I get there? "Quite easy," said my caller, "You know Abbott Road." I said I knew Abbott Road. It's a residential street that runs between Brunswick Road and East India Dock. I couldn't remember any shops in it. When I mentioned this, my caller explained that it wasn't a shop deal. "A person-to-person transaction. The man you want is called Chelford. Dick Chelford. His house is half way along, in Barwick Close. That's a turning to the right off Abbott Road. Number 17 Barwick Close. All right?" I said that was clear enough, and to tell him that I'd be right along and that I'd have my cheque book with me. Mr Robinson didn't seem to like that. He said that it'd be better if I made it cash.

'The asking price was £500 and I don't carry cash like that about with me. However, I said I could call in at the bank on the way there. If I telephoned them, they could have the money ready for me.

'Mr Robinson said, "Excellent. You do that," and rang off. So I set out, confident that I'd have no difficulty finding this Mr Chelford. I drew the cash all right, but after that the trouble started. For though I plodded, more than once, up and down Abbott Road I could not find any turning off it called Barwick Close. In fact, there was only one turning on the right, a cul-de-sac called Bagwell Passage, and no turning of any sort on the left. When I stopped other pedestrians to enquire, they were perfectly prepared to be helpful, but united in saying that they had never heard of Barwick Close. So far as they knew there was no street of that name in the neighbourhood. I thought the only thing to do was to go back to my office and telephone Mr Robinson for further and better particulars. It was at this point that I realised that I hadn't asked him for his telephone number or his address. No matter. He would be in the telephone book, doubtless with fifty other Robinsons. But when I did get back there was no question of telephoning him or anyone else. The fire brigade was in possession, and I had other things to think about.'

At this point, the actual attendance note finished, but Tara had added a comment of her own.

'I asked Colin at what time the telephone call from Mr Robinson had come. He said,

"Around two o'clock, or just before," and that gave me an opening to put to him a statement made by a witness called Father Mawden to the effect that, as he went past the shop *at about half past two* he had seen Colin coming out of the passage-way beside it. His actual expression was that Colin had been "slinking out," and that when Colin saw him he made off down the street without looking back.

"'Totally untrue," Colin assured me. "When I left the shop to look for Barwick Close, I was in too much of a hurry to hang about. And when I got back, the fire brigade was already busy.'"

'Not really very helpful,' said Fearne. 'I've called a full partners' meeting for ten o'clock tomorrow. That will give them time to read the paper. One point first. Who has been acting for Colin up to now?'

'I asked Alison. She said it was a solicitor called Graveway. A one man firm. He didn't seem up to the job. His main objective seemed to be not to upset the judge. Alison had insisted on their changing to us. To start with Colin wasn't too keen. A business friend had recommended Graveway. He didn't want to upset him. But in the end he agreed.'

'Sounds as though his wife rules the roost,' said Fearne. 'I'll have to see what my partners say about it.'

At their meeting next morning, it soon became clear that there were two schools of thought. Hugo and Tara were willing to take on the job. They knew and distrusted Max Graveway and were very willing to wipe his eye. Neither of the two senior partners was keen, but they didn't feel strongly enough about it to overrule their ardent juniors. Mr Piggin, who was present, had remained silent throughout.

When the matter had been discussed from every possible point of view, Fearne summed up.

He said, 'All right. We'll take it on. I'll apply to the court for a fifteen day postponement. With a change of legal representation they're bound to grant that. I think it would be a mistake to ask for longer. But it will mean that we've all got to get busy. And quickly. So, we split the job. Bob, can you look into the financial side of it? If Colin was on the verge of bankruptcy that could have offered him an inducement to burn down the shop and collect the insurance money.'

'I can do that,' said Bob. 'Was the shop under-insured or over-insured? Was the policy recent or long standing? That sort of thing.'

'Could all be useful. And you, Hugo, might look into the incendiary side of it. You have got friends in the fire brigade I believe.'

'The ones who play rugger you mean. Yes. I could tackle them. It will have to be done discreetly.'

'And you, Tara, have another word with Alison and see what you can dig out. In particular the names of any possible rivals. People in whose interest it would be to put Colin out of business.'

Tara said she could do that. She was pleased that the affair was being taken seriously.

'And that,' said Fearne, 'brings us to the heart of the matter. The important, but irritating, Father Mawden. Until we can shake his evidence, or at least cast some doubt on it, we're in trouble. Piggy, do you think you—'

'I had a feeling that would be landed on me,' said Mr Piggin, with a smile. He didn't add—I do all the dirty work—but it was clearly what he meant.

'You can have Michael Donovan to help you.'

Michael was a precocious youth, of uncertain age. When school attendance officers threatened, he claimed to be seventeen, and produced a crumpled and almost illegible birth certificate in support of this claim. Fearne thought that he could assume any age between twelve and eighteen according to the requirements of the moment. He had not investigated the matter too closely. Office boys were not easy to get and Michael seemed to work very happily under the wing of Mr Piggin. He was respectful to the two senior partners and tolerated the two juniors.

'Very well,' said Fearne. 'Get stuck in. I'll re-convene this meeting for the same time next Monday. When we hear what you've got to say, we can make up our minds about further steps.'

At their next meeting, Bob Bracknell spoke first. He said, 'In many ways I had the easiest job. I know Simon Hendrix, who audits the Blakely accounts. He showed me their last three years' tax returns. Nothing to hide and nothing to be ashamed of. One medium sized fire insurance policy, taken out some years ago and not increased since, though, Simon says, it should have been because they were making steady progress. Increasing sales, increasing stocks.'

'So, really, they're now under-insured.'

'You could say so. And that makes it extremely unlikely that Blakely was so short of money that he'd be tempted to go in for an insurance swindle.'

'Unlikely,' agreed Fearne. 'But not impossible. He might have had some urgent private debt that had to be settled against time.'

'Possible,' said Bob, 'but personally I'd need a good deal of convincing.'

'Hugo?'

'I talked about it with one of my friends in the Volunteer Fire Brigade. They're an uninhibited crowd.'

Fearne knew about the V.F.B. Most of its

members played for one or other of the local rugger clubs. It was widely held that if your premises caught fire it was, on the whole less damaging to them to let the fire burn itself out than to call in the enthusiastic amateur fire fighters.

'Exaggerated nonsense,' said Hugo. 'They've done a lot of good work in their time. And I reckon that the chap I was talking to—Jesse Collins—knows as much about fires—how and why they start—as anybody in London. He explained to me about that old alarm clock they found among the debris in the burnt out store. I couldn't entirely follow it, but it seems what you do is run one of the flexes from an electric fire through the clock, having turned the fire off, of course, strip the insulation and bring the ends out through the face of the clock. O.K.'

'With you so far,' said Fearne, who had been making a sketch as Hugo talked.

'Then lay the fire down on its back with a lot of inflammable stuff over it. When the hour hand reaches the point you've settled on, it forms a junction with the bared ends of the wires, which turns the fire on, and up she goes.'

'Then what you're telling me is that it doesn't need great expertise, or one of those delayed action fuses. I mean the sort of gadget the S.A.S. used in the war when they were destroying enemy planes on the ground.'

184

'Nothing like that. It's the sort of thing anyone who knew what he was doing could rig up in five or ten minutes. However, he did make one point that might help us. He said that in almost all the fires he had investigated, where arson was suspected, they usually found at least two, sometimes three or four, different points of origin. I suppose an arsonist doesn't want there to be any chance of the fire being put out before it gets going. So, if they detect more than one point of origin, that's something they always report to the insurers.'

'You mean because it negates any suggestion that the fire was accidental.'

'Right. You don't find four or five accidents happening in different places at the same time.' Fearne thought about this.

He said, 'It's a sort of argument. Since, in this case there's only one point of origin the fire could have been accidental. But it doesn't explain the clock.

'Surely the clock's decisive,' said Tara. She was tired of listening to her seniors bumbling on about something that seemed absolutely clear to her. 'If Colin was, in fact, arranging to set fire to his own place he wouldn't need anything like that. He'd just light a candle in a plate full of old film and take himself off. An intruder couldn't risk doing anything as simple as that. He'd need an arrangement that gave him an absolutely accurate timing

185

for the start of the fire. Then he could be sure that he could manoeuvre Colin to be out of the way, on a fool's errand, when the fire started.'

Bob said, 'I can see counsel picking a lot of holes in that line of argument. The fact is that the clock fits both versions. Colin could have rigged it up and departed, knowing that it gave him plenty of time to get to Abbott Road and keep out of the way. Or an outsider could have waited until he saw Colin leave, slipped in, and fixed things up.'

'Fifty-fifty,' said Fearne. 'Tara?'

Tara said, 'What I particularly wanted to find out from Alison was whether she had any idea of who could want to put ALL GEAR out of business. Somehow I couldn't see any of the large well known sports shops doing such a thing, but I did find a very possible candidate. It isn't a sports shop, it's a keep fit crowd.

'Twenty or thirty kids who meet at a local gym, run by a man called Bob Blacking. He's got two assistants, both ex-army P.T. instructors. He's set up his own shop in the gym. To start with, it just sold P.T. kits, but lately he's branched out into sports gear. Footballs, cricket bats, that sort of thing. He made a little money that way from the kids in his own group, but soon found out that most of their parents preferred to buy from ALL GEAR. Better choice of stuff, they said. So, if you're looking for a number one suspect, I'd pick Blacking, or maybe one or other of his assistants, Stanley and Leonard. Known to the boys as Stan-the-man and Len-the-lump.'

'They sound a likely trio of villains,' agreed Fearne. 'But unfortunately it wasn't one of them that Father Mawden says he saw slipping out of the shop.'

'Right. And I did find out a bit about Father Mawden. Seems he acts as unofficial chaplain to the group. Blacking thinks a lot of him. A great help, and totally reliable, so he says.'

'Which is just what we *didn't* want to hear,' said Bob. 'We want him to be unreliable. If he's to be trusted, and he really did see Colin slinking out of the shop at half past two on the afternoon of the fire, then we're up against it. You've talked to Mawden more than once in the last few days haven't you Piggy? What did you make of him?'

Mr Piggin, who had been unusually silent, thought about this for almost a minute before answering.

Then he said, 'He's not an easy man to sum up. First things first. He's not a clergyman. At least, not of the established church. When I pressed him on the point he said something about a group called Ninth Day Adventists, whose doctrine he professed to follow.'

'Isn't that dishonest?' said Tara. 'To call himself "Father".'

'Not really. You're not claiming any special

187

status, in law, by allowing people to call you "Father", or "Daddy", or "Pater". And the people I talked to seemed to approve of him. Having no particular church or congregation to look after means he's got a lot of spare time. As well as acting as spiritual adviser to the gymnasts, he does a number of unofficial, and unpaid, jobs. He was in charge of the Christmas collection for the Hospice, and he ran two boys' camps last summer. When I couldn't get very far with him on my own, it occurred to me that perhaps I was approaching him from the wrong angle. Or, rather, at the wrong level. Instead of trying to get at him through his colleagues, what I ought to be doing was find out what the boys really thought of him.'

'How did you propose to do that?'

'By using a boy. Michael Donovan has done a number of jobs for me in the past and I've always found him reliable, so I thought I'd slip him into this gymnasium crowd to see if he could ferret out anything.'

'And has he?'

'Early days. He's taken the first step. I put him in funds to pay the very modest entrance fee and he's now been enrolled as a member, and has attended, rather reluctantly, a number of P.T. classes. Physical jerks are not really his line, but he's kept his eyes and his ears open. I'm expecting a report from him this evening.'

'Seems O.K. to me,' said Donovan. 'Too bloody energetic for my taste, but quite straightforward. A friendly crowd, on the whole. Two I've got to know best are Rufus Penny, so called because of a mop of red hair, and his kid brother, Dave. I've had one or two drinking sessions with them. If there is anything funny going on, they'll open up about it, sooner or later.'

'Do they know you work here? I notice you haven't been to the office for the last week or two.'

'I thought it would be better not to let on that I had any connection with the law. When I signed up for the gym class I put my name down as Pierce. When Blacking wanted to know what I did, I said that I had worked for you once, but that I'd been sacked on suspicion of fiddling the petty cash, and since then I'd been hanging round looking for a job. I told him I was living, rent free, with my auntie, and that was my address if anyone wanted to write to me. No good telephoning her, I said, she's deaf as a post. I've warned her letters might be coming, addressed to Michael Pierce. She knows I'm up to something, but she won't give me away. She's a crafty old witch, with a sideline in shoplifting. I don't mean that she steals stuff herself, but she organises the disposal side.'

Piggin thought about this.

It seemed to him that his assistant had organised his background with some skill, and he congratulated him on the care he had taken. He added, 'Just now you said, *if* there's something funny going on. Have you any reason to think there might be?'

'If there is, it's something Blacking, Stan and Len know about, but it isn't common knowledge.'

'What sort of thing?'

'Difficult to explain. It's not so much what they say, as what they don't say. It could be something serious, or it could be a joke. But I'm pretty sure I'll get it from Rufus sooner or later, at one of our evening piss-ups. More than once he's been on the point of telling me, then he's thought better of it and kept his mouth shut.'

'You said "sooner or later",' said Mr Piggin. 'Make it sooner, if you can. And meanwhile, for Christ's sake, *watch your step.*'

He was beginning to wonder what he had let his young assistant in for.

*　　*　　*

Michael Donovan, who had a prudent regard for his own well being, had made a careful inspection of the building of which the gym formed part. He had done this with an eye to

190

the possibility that he might, at some future time, be anxious to leave it hurriedly and inconspicuously. It was a curious edifice.

The gymnasium itself was a single large room at first floor level. The main approach to it, from the front, was a short flight of steps which crossed the ditch that separated the building from the road and led to a rather handsome pair of doors.

This was the entrance reserved to the proprietors, Blacking and his two assistants, and was available to important visitors. Blacking locked the doors carefully after each time it was used.

There were windows on either side of this front entrance and four more in the wall on the facing side. All six were covered externally by wire mesh. This diminished the light they let through, but protected them from the attentions of the local young who were accustomed to throwing stones through any window within their range. Windows so guarded, he realised, offered no prospect for surreptitious entrance or exit, which was a pity.

The boys used a door at the back of the building which opened on to a corridor, from which a flight of steps led up to the gym. There were doors on both sides of this corridor. Three on the right, the first of which was a lavatory, the second a shower room—a cramped affair, which so rarely produced hot water that boys normally went home to wash and change after their efforts in the gym. The third door on that side was a large cupboard, probably designed for brooms and cleaning material, but now used as a depository for unwanted junk.

The doors on the other side were more important.

The first led to a reception room, where Blacking interviewed the parents of prospective gymnasts. The second to what might have been described as the control room. The walls were lined with bookshelves which flanked a large safe. The only furniture was an impressive looking partners desk. Behind it was a range of switch boxes and fuses, and beside it, hitched up out of harm's way, the rope which swung the alarm bell in the roof.

Donovan, being one of the few boys who chose to suffer a cold and cramped shower after gym, found it easy enough to arrange to be the last boy left behind. The only obstacle to further exploration was the tiresome fact that Rufus and Dave Penny seemed to be so attracted by his personality and conversation, that they usually stayed behind, too.

Making a virtue of necessity, Donovan had got them to help him clear out the broom cupboard. Most of the contents could be stowed under the stairs. The remaining boxes were arranged as seats and a table, and there they spent comfortable and private evenings, smoking and drinking tinned lager bought with money—this was not revealed—supplied by Mr Piggin.

The next and vital step was to secure an emergency exit, in case the powers-that-be descended on them.

This was not difficult. The door at the far end of the corridor led to a path which ran round the back of the building and out to the road. This door was supposed to be kept locked too, but the key had, more than once, been left in the lock. Which was right up Donovan's street. Using a cake of soap, he had produced an accurate impression of the key, from which one of Mr Piggin's friends had manufactured a duplicate, which Donovan kept carefully to hand.

He felt certain, as he told Mr Piggin, that in one of their cosy evening sessions, Rufus would eventually hand him the secret he was angling for. When it did happen, it was, none the less, a surprise, amounting almost to a shock.

On that occasion Rufus, who was clearly worried about something, had been unusually silent, and Donovan had been driven to make most of the conversation. Finally, in an effort to introduce some topic that might interest his hearer, he had mentioned Father Mawden.

'Seems a friendly sort of chap,' he said.

Turning round on him sharply Rufus had

said, 'Don't let him get too friendly.'

'Why? Oh. I see. You mean he's one of that sort—'

'Very much one of that sort,' said Rufus grimly. 'Let him get you alone, with the door locked, and he'd soon have your trousers down.'

'Is that true, or just something people say about him?'

'Not a lot of people know about it, or they wouldn't let their sons come here. But it's bible truth. You remember that silly kid, the one called Flossie? And there were two others, Paki boys, Ali and Dino. Mawden was caught at it with one of them, by Len.'

'And I suppose he reported him to Blacking.'

'Of course.'

'Then why wasn't something done about it? I mean to say, it's a criminal offence. Something he could have been jugged for.' And when Rufus said nothing. 'Isn't it?'

'It certainly is. And I don't know for certain why Blacking did nothing about it. But that doesn't mean I can't guess. He thought that if he didn't report it, and ordered the three boys concerned to say nothing about it, he'd have no difficulty in terrifying them into silence. It could be useful to have Mawden under his thumb. He saw that he might be useful. In a lot of ways.'

'And was he?' said Donovan.

The silence in the little underground room seemed to be waiting, breathlessly, for an answer. In the end, when it did come, it opened a lot of doors that had been shut before.

'He surely was useful,' said Rufus slowly. 'When Blacking and his friends decided to torch the ALL GEAR shop which was attracting away a lot of their custom, they were able to force Mawden to go in and set up the fire arrangement for them, while they organised useful alibis for themselves. More than that. They forced him to say that he had seen Blakely sneaking away from the place. Jam for them on both sides of the bread.'

'Yes. I see.'

So now the truth had come up and was staring him full in the face.

Rufus said, 'You're pretty friendly with that lawyer. What's he called, Piggin, aren't you?'

'Yes. I shall have to tell him what you've just told me.'

'Tell him as soon as you can. And what's more, you'd better ask him to arrange to have you looked after.'

'Why do you say that?' asked Donovan, his mouth dry.

'My kid brother told me, this evening, that they were on to you. Seems they followed you yesterday and found that you were still in with your old firm, and that story about you being sacked for pinching cash was boloney. He heard them talking about it. Seems the idea was to come along one evening, take us up to the top storey, and chuck us out of the window. The cover story would be that we were fooling round, climbing out, and had slipped. When he told me that, I had to put you on your guard.'

'Well, thank you for that,' said Donovan. 'I do see I shall have to be careful.'

In the silence that followed, they both heard it.

The click, as the main door to the gym was unlocked and shut again. And the sound of three sets of feet. Rufus was already out of the cupboard.

'Time we were shifting,' he said urgently.

They tip-toed along the corridor.

'You got your key? Right. Come on.'

The three men who had come into the gym had stopped moving, and they could hear the sound of their voices. Blacking seemed to be giving orders to his assistants. They could guess, only too easily, what those orders were.

It was at this point that Donovan discovered, in a moment of shocked horror that the door was not only locked, they could deal with that, as they had done many times before, but that on this occasion the key had been left in the lock on the other side, blocking it.

After two frantic and unsuccessful attempts to get his own key into the lock, Donovan caught a glimpse of his friend's white and anguished face. It was a look that should have paralysed him. In fact it spurred him to rapid action. He abandoned his futile attack on the locked door, and stepped away from it, back into the corridor, with a silent prayer that the door into the control room might have been left unlocked.

Which it had.

He flung the door open, darted into the room and jumped on to the desk. Then, reaching up, he unhooked the rope of the alarm bell, and shouting to Rufus to help, swung on it with all his strength.

Up in the roof the bell started to sound its brazen warning to the world.

*   *   *

To Mr Piggin, Fearne said, 'When the fire brigade and the police arrived on the scene together, we explained that your boy, Donovan, and a friend of his, had stayed behind after gym, found themselves locked in, and panicked. We offered them a call-out fee, which they were glad to accept. I considered that it was money well spent.'

Mr Piggin agreed. He considered that it was money very well spent.

Three weeks had elapsed and he was more than satisfied with the way things had fallen out. What Michael Donovan had discovered about Father Mawden had made him totally ineffective as a witness in support of the fire-raisers. More than useless. If they played their cards right, dangerous. For what Fearne had done was to apply to the court for leave to call three more witnesses. The boy called Flossie and the two Pakis.

When Father Mawden was told about this, as he had to be, he realised that his secret was going to come out. Indeed it was not simply going to come out. It was going to be accorded the fullest and most painful publicity, greedily lapped up by the press and the public, as the new witnesses were examined and cross-examined. Which was why he had taken his own life.

Fearne said, 'And it's clear that he had decided to wipe the slate clean. Seeing that he left behind a full statement, signed and witnessed and addressed to the Coroner, which was not only a confession of his own part in the matter, but also incriminated Blacking and his two assistants.'

'Satisfactory for us,' agreed Mr Piggin.

The Crown, having lost the only witness who involved Colin Blakely in the fire-raising, had abandoned the prosecution, and had turned their minds to the question of whether, in its place, a successful prosecution could be mounted against Blacking and his assistants.

This was more difficult.

The Crown Prosecution Service looked at

the evidence and didn't think much of it. The verdict on Father Mawden had been that he had taken his own life while the balance of his mind was disturbed. This afforded a golden opportunity to the defence to cast doubt on his written statement. If the balance of his mind was officially agreed to be disturbed, how could anything he said or wrote be taken seriously?

Worse, backed by their families, all three boys staunchly refused to give evidence.

The upshot had been that Blacking and his two assistants, who had been free on bail, were now informed that no prosecution was to follow. They were nevertheless advised to make themselves scarce. Which they were glad to do, by the simple process of taking themselves off to friends in Ireland.

'Meanwhile,' said Fearne, 'as a result of all this, the gymnasium class has dispersed. In most cases, I don't doubt, to the relief of their parents who were beginning to get worried by the stories that were being circulated.'

'And no doubt,' said Mr Piggin, 'they approved of the new use to which the gym was being put.'

The District Council, who owned the building, had leased it, when it fell vacant, to a local dramatic group. They had installed a stage and seating and were now engaged in an acrimonious dispute as to whether the Christmas pantomime should be 'Ali Baba and the Forty Thieves', or 'Robinson Crusoe and his Girl Friday'.

Fearne, hearing about this, knew that things were now, happily, back to normal. It afforded him a moment to consider the events of the last few weeks calmly. He said to Mr Piggin, 'A lot of the credit must go to your young assistant. Which leads me to suggest that it's about time he became an established member of the firm. We've got plenty of room for a second managing clerk.'

'Certainly. But I warn you. If you let him in, he'll soon be taking over as senior partner.'

Y MYNYDDOED SANCTIAIDD

Dai Morgan was the ideal walking companion. He was twenty years older than me, but much fitter, and he was not only a good walker, he was a good talker. He had crammed a lot of experience into sixty-five years of living.

When he'd finished his service in the Royal Navy as a C.P.O. he'd joined the Liverpool Docks Police. After that he had been Chief Security Officer for Carfrae, the Shippers, and could, no doubt, have retired on his pension at sixty. However, he had decided that life had more to offer and had become a probation officer. He was neither sentimental nor cynical about the job. I sometimes thought that if we had a few more probation officers like Dai there would be less juvenile crime.

On this occasion we started at Porthmadog and set off north easterly across the Cambrian Mountains and the Clwydian Range. We covered twenty-five miles on the first day, and nearly thirty on the second, finishing at a cottage at Llangwypan, a village at the end of a road that led to nowhere. There was no difficulty about lodging. Dai had worked for most of the courts along the North coast of Wales, from Bangor to Flint. Old Mrs

Philpott, who owned the cottage, knew him well. As we sat in her parlour, happily relaxed after our exertions, I could sniff the supper she was cooking for us.

The sun was going down behind the odd shaped mountains, hump-backed like a line of camels. Dai said, 'You're looking at Y Mynyddoed Sanctiaidd.'

'Meaning what?'

'Come on, boyo. You've lived five years in Swansea. Haven't you got your tongue round our beautiful language?'

'I can order a pint of beer, and I can shout "Put the boot in, Llanelli."'

'Shame on you, Y Mynyddoed Sanctiaidd are the Holy Mountains.'

'What's holy about them?' I said. They looked much like the other hills we had trudged over that day.

'I've no idea. Probably some holy man lived and died up there.'

I had a feeling that there was more to it than that, so I waited. In the end Dai said, 'They're holy to me for a particular reason.' There was another pause. I could hear the clatter of pans in the kitchen. If our meal had come in then I should never have heard about Carwyn.

'It was one of my first jobs,' said Dai. 'My Superintendent was a nice man called Hubble. Known to everyone in the service as Hubble-bubble. Not a fool, by any means. He said, "This lad Carwyn. He's on remand until

Monday. I want you to pick him up and take him to Court. I've had a word with the magistrate and he's agreed to commit him to the Probation Hostel at Prestatyn. You can take him there by rail."

'"If he's on remand I imagine he's already at the Police Station, or did they send him home?"

'"Neither. He's at my house. He's been there for the last week."

'This surprised me. It is not normally part of the duties of a probation officer to house delinquent children.'

'"It's an odd case altogether," said Hubble. "He was offered the chance of going home, but he refused. He said he'd rather stay in prison. That's when I offered to look after him."

'"Might he have been scared of his parents?"

'"He's got no parents. He's been looked after by his aunt since his mother died five years ago. She was in Court at the first hearing. She didn't look to me like the sort of woman a child would be afraid of. It might have been her husband. He's said to be a hard case. I haven't been able to find out much about him yet."

'The Liverpool magistrate's Court is in the Town Hall by the Royal Liver Building. The Clerk was an old friend. He said, "It seems the boy's uncle got him a job with Curleys, the

Estate Agents, in Chester Street. It was only an office boy job, but you have to start somewhere, and they liked the look of him. Then, on his first Friday there, he helped himself to a couple of pound notes out of the petty cash, and did it so clumsily that one of the girls saw him, and reported him. He didn't even trouble to deny it. Of course, they had to run him in."

'It sounded odd to the magistrate, too. He gave us the promised probation order. So far Carwyn hadn't opened his mouth, and I hadn't tried to talk to him, because that usually shuts them up worse than before. He was a silent child. I suppose his age must have been given as sixteen or he wouldn't have got a job, but he didn't look much more than twelve. His face was whitish for a boy who had spent the last five years on a farm in the country, but the overall impression I got was of sadness. He really was the saddest looking boy I had ever seen. I don't mean that he was crying or complaining. But he had those dark inward looking eyes that Welsh children sometimes have, and he seemed to be spending most of his time thinking about life and finding it hollow.

'It's a ninety minutes run from Liverpool to Prestatyn. We had the carriage to ourselves, and I was relieved, if a mite surprised, when he opened the conversation. He said, "Have you ever known a lion eat straw?"

204

'I said, "I don't know a lot about lions. I saw one or two in Africa. When I was in the Navy."

'"Do you think they'd eat straw?"

'"More usually they ate other animals."

'"That's what I thought."

'He sat for a moment looking out of the window. I feared that our conversation might be at an end. No. He was assembling his ideas.

'"Have you ever seen a leopard?"

'"Only in the zoo."

'"Would one lie down with kids?"

'"Certainly. Even the fiercest animals are friendly with their own children."

'He thought about this, but decided to pass it up. He said, "Do you know what a cockatrice is?"

'I had an idea where we were going now. I said, "I always thought of it as something like a scorpion."

'"I guessed it might be something like that. Do you think a wolf and a lamb could lie down together?"

'Thanks to a strict Chapel upbringing I was on grid by this time.

'I said, "Book of Isaiah. Right?"

'"I heard it in Church on Sunday. Mr Hubble took me. It seemed funny when I heard it but I've been thinking about it. Lots of animals who are supposed to be enemies aren't really. We had a dog and a cat would curl up together on the rug by the fire. So I suppose a wolf and a lamb might hit it off."

"'I think it would depend on how hungry the wolf was."

'He didn't like this. He said reproachfully, "The Bible didn't say it would work any old place. Just when they were in the Holy Mountains. It's what they call the mountains where I live, see?"

'I remembered then that his address had been given as Waen. Incidentally, you can see them from that window.'

I got up to have a look. The sun was on its way down. I was beginning to be interested in Carwyn. 'Did he say anything else?'

'Nothing until we were getting near Prestatyn. Then he said, "I could believe the animals lying down together. It was the lion eating straw that worried me. It seemed funny somehow." And he smiled, just that once.

'When I handed him over to the Superintendent of the Hostel I said, "I don't think you'll have much trouble with this number."

'The Superintendent, who seemed to have taken to him at sight, said, "Fine. We'll put him in the gardening squad."

'When I got back to Liverpool I walked round to Chester Street. It's a sad place because it was one of the business centres of Liverpool, but it was dying. The only buildings in use were a big office block on the corner, then Curley's office, then a derelict and

206

boarded up structure. Then the Bank and a few shops. I knew Bill Armitage, the Senior Partner in Curleys, quite well from my time with the Shipping Company.

'He said, "It's the oddest case I've ever met. The boy came here on the Monday. His aunt brought him. A bit down in the mouth, I thought, but natural if it was his first job away from home. Then, on Friday, he helps himself out of the petty cash, as cool as you please. You could almost have said he wanted to be found out."

'"Might he have been protecting himself?"

'"What from?"

'"I don't know. But he refused to go home between the two hearings."

'"His aunt didn't look like a dragon. I got the impression they were very fond of each other. Maybe it's the uncle."

'"He seems to be the mystery man in the case", I agreed. Then I had to get on with half a dozen other jobs that Hubble had ready for me. It was on the Thursday of that week that he said, "I've just heard Carwyn's decamped. Can you find out what's happened, and cope with it."

'Those were the sort of instructions you get in the probation service. I telephoned the Superintendent. He sounded upset. He said, "I haven't got the whole story yet. You know how these boys clam up. But what I understand happened was that two men drove up in a car, forced their way through the hedge at the bottom of the garden, and Carwyn went off with them."

'"Willingly?"

'"That's just what I don't know."

'I said, "If he's gone anywhere it'll be his aunt's house. I'd better get out there quick."

'I'd found out the name of the aunt by now. It was Thomas. Like a million other people in Wales. Rebecca Thomas lived on this steading outside Waen. It was a modest place, with a run of chicken houses, well protected against the foxes, and a few cows in the field. The sort of place a woman could just manage, particularly if she had a boy to help her.

'She was in her working clothes, not the smart gear she'd worn to Court. She seemed to be expecting me, but there was something in her attitude, something I couldn't, at that moment, unriddle. It was when she led the way into the parlour that the shock hit me.

'There was a photograph on the side board. It was a good photograph, and I could see it very clearly. Two men, head and shoulders. I recognised them at once. You don't forget a face when you have seen it behind a sawn-off shot gun, and had plenty of opportunity to study it later in Court.

'The Procter brothers, Malvyn and Tam, had broken into the bonded warehouse of the Carfrae Shipping firm. We got a last-minute tip off and I arrived with the police at the moment they were making off. They had tried to shoot it out, but had been outgunned. One of the policemen was badly wounded. One of them slightly. The Procters got ten years. I did some rapid arithmetic. With full remission, they could both have been out, but only for a month or so.

'Mrs Thomas must have seen me looking at the photograph. She said, without a trace of feeling in her voice, "Mal is my husband. I changed my name when he went inside."

'I took a deep breath and said, "Tell me, Mrs Thomas, what have they done with Carwyn?"

'As I said that she crumpled up. There is no other word to describe it. Then she started to cry, quite gently. It went on for a long time, whilst I sat looking at her. Then she dried her eyes and started to talk.

'As soon as I got back to Liverpool I had a word with Jack Solomon. He was head of the Liverpool Special Crimes Squad.

'I said, "I've reason to believe that the Procter brothers and two of their friends are underneath the branch of the Home Counties Bank in Chester Street at this moment waiting for it to close on Friday evening, so that they can get busy on the inner wall of the strong room."

'"You don't often talk nonsense," said Jack. "Tell me how they'd get there. And don't suggest they broke into the derelict house next door. It's guarded as strongly as the Bank."

"'They didn't bother. They put this kid Carwyn into Curley's office to scout the way to the cellar and get copies of the keys. They let themselves in there on Wednesday night, and were under the empty house by Thursday morning with everything cleared up behind them."

"'And just how do you know this?"

"'Mal miscalculated. He didn't realise how fond a lonely woman could get of a lonely boy."

'Jack thought about this. He said, "I take it, then, that what Carwyn did was to protect himself."

"'That's right. He wanted to put himself in baulk. I doubt if he intended to split, but they couldn't take a chance on it. That was their second mistake."

The story seemed to be at an end. I said, 'Go on. What happened?'

'Oh, they laid for them at the Bank. The Procters tried to use their guns. This time the police weren't pulling any punches. Mal was killed. Thomas died that night in hospital. The other two didn't resist. They got five years.'

The way he said it didn't make it sound important. I knew he was thinking about Carwyn.

I said, 'Did they find the boy?'

210

Dai was staring out of the window. There was a glow in the sky. A colour you sometimes get in hilly country, difficult to describe, more green than pink. There were still a few small cushion-shaped clouds hanging stationary over the tops, and the sun, as it went down, was starting to throw long shadows into the corries.

'He's up there somewhere,' said Dai softly. 'I'd guess he's happy now, with the tigers and the kids and the wolves and lambs all playing together on the holy mountains. Maybe he's found out by now whether lions do eat straw when they're hungry.'

The lady of the house came in with a loaded tray. She said, 'What's that you're talking about Mr Morgan, some nonsense. Lions is it?'

'Just a bit of nonsense, Mrs Philpott. What's under that dish. It smells good.'

THE KLAGENFURT TOTE

When I got a signal to report at Divisional Headquarters at Klagenfurt, I felt no misgiving. Not the slightest premonition of danger. I drove myself in a nice little biscuit-coloured Steyr, picked up near Villach a week before. The war in Europe was just over. True, there was still a bit of nonsense going on in South East Asia, but only the professional soldiers worried about that. For the time being we were on holiday.

Fifteen minutes later I was talking to the G.S.O.2 at Division. He had thick black hair, a brown face, a faded D.S.O. and a smooth manner.

'I expect you're wondering why we picked on you,' he said.

I said, 'Yes.'

'Well, there's obviously a mathematical side to it, if you see what I mean. It's going to mean doing a bit of calculation, and doing it fast, and getting it right.'

'I wondered if, perhaps, the Engineers—'

'Oh, certainly. You'll have all the sapper help you want. They're going to put it up for you. In fact, we've chosen the site already.'

'What is it they're going to put up?' I asked.

'A Tote.'

'I'm not a racing man,' I said. 'I wonder if

you could explain just how a Tote *works*.'

'Well—I'm not sure that I know. I've lost a lot of money on them in my time—'

I could visualize him, without difficulty, in well-cut hacking jacket, at a pre-war point-to-point.

'But the principle of the thing's straightforward enough. All you have to do is to calculate how much money has been staked on each horse, and how much on the race as a whole. That gives you the odds. If there's a thousand pounds in total stake money, and a hundred pounds on a particular horse—'

'Ten to one,' I said. 'I can do that.'

'Well, no. Nine to one. You've got to let them have their stake back. And then there's the ten per cent cut for the management. We want to make something out of this for Army funds.'

'In a real Tote,' I said thoughtfully, 'I suppose there's quite a lot of machinery. Gadgets and so on, which do calculations like that automatically.'

'I expect so. We can't run to anything like that. But you can have as much help as you need. We're building it big enough to hold a hundred men. That should be enough, I expect.'

'More than enough,' I said.

On my way home I stopped at Regimental Headquarters. The C.O. saw me coming, but too late to dodge into his caravan.

'Why,' I said, 'pick on me?'

Like all successful C.O.s he was, at heart, a diplomat.

'It's a terrific compliment,' he said. 'Dick McCreery's very keen to make the meeting a success.'

I said that I knew that the Eighth Army Commander was an amateur jockey of note. There were three cavalry regiments in our Division, and any number of horses, mostly taken over from the recently disbanded Independent Cossack Brigade. That much made sense. But why the Tote?

'But it's a brilliant idea,' said the C.O. 'Almost everyone in the Army's got his pockets full of money which—well, I don't exactly say loot, but he'd hate to have to explain too carefully where it came from.'

'True,' I said.

'Well, here's a ready-made, water-tight explanation. "I won it on the Tote." I don't suggest,' he added hurriedly, 'that the General thought it out in precisely that way. But it's an aspect we mustn't lose sight of.'

'All right,' I said. 'A hundred men. It'll be easier to control it if we keep it within the Regiment.'

'Thirty from each Battery and ten from R.H.Q.,' said the C.O. automatically.

'Just one more thing. I suppose there'll be other, bigger and better race meetings after this. And bigger and better Totes. I don't want to get stuck as permanent Tote Officer to the Division.'

'If you get away with this one, someone else shall do the next. In fact, Hubert had better act as your second-in-command. Then *he* can do the next one. And so on.'

'My God,' said Hubert, when I broke the news to him. 'I've never been on a racecourse in my life.'

'It's quite simple,' I said. 'You just count up all the money that's been invested on each horse, and divide it into the total less ten per cent for the Tote.'

It was certainly a lovely racecourse. A stretch of meadowland lying above the summer-low Drava, bordered by dusty hedges and shaded by broad oaks. Put it down anywhere in the shires, it wouldn't have looked out of place. The white rail was nearly completed.

And the Tote.

This was a large, square structure, with eighteen pigeon-holes, six on each of three sides. Twelve of them said 'STAKE HERE', three said 'COLLECT HERE', two said 'CHANGE GIVEN', and one said 'COMPLAINTS'.

In the centre was a sort of small pagoda.

'You sit there,' said Hubert, 'and declare the odds.' I could visualize the scene only too clearly.

'You sit right beside me,' I said, 'and check

up everything I do. Now let's think how we'll organize it. Seventeen cashiers and seventeen checkers. Seventeen adders and seventeen runners.'

'Who shall we put in complaints?'

'The Sergeant-Major. And we shall want at least one full rehearsal. The races are the day after tomorrow. Better lay one on for tomorrow afternoon.'

*   *   *

The rehearsal went with surprising smoothness. A dozen 'extras' circled round the outside of the Tote, laying imaginary bets on nonexistent horses. The cashiers raked in the phantom money, the checkers checked, the adders added, the runners ran, and I declared some confident odds.

That evening the Sergeant-Major came to see me.

'Everything went very nicely this afternoon,' I said.

'Yes, sir,' said the Sergeant-Major. But there was something on his mind.

'What is it?' I said.

'It's the only fatigue I've ever laid on,' said the Sergeant-Major, inconsequently, 'where I got more volunteers than I needed. I did hear'—he lowered his voice (thus ceasing to be audible the other side of the square)—'that places on it were changing hands at five pounds each.'

'Have you heard anything else?' I said.

'Well, sir. Coming back from the course in the three-tonner, I was sitting beside the driver. I wasn't listening, but you know how you can't help overhearing what's said in the back. It was Thomas—the one who's a bookmaker's runner in civvy street—and he was saying to Whitehair: "They just hand you money through that little hole, eh?" and Whitehair said: "That's right." And Thomas said: "When you think you've got enough, you go and tell someone how much you've got," and Whitehair said: "You've got it."'

'And what did Thomas say to that?'

'He didn't say anything, sir. He just laughed. They both laughed.'

'I can see,' I said, 'that I must take steps to protect their characters. I want you to organize this for me, Sergeant-Major. Will you lay on a hundred sandbags, each one with a label fastened to it. And I particularly don't want a lot of gossip about it.'

'In that case,' said the Sergeant-Major, 'I'd better do it myself.'

'Put 'em in my car at the last moment before we drive down to the course.'

*   *   *

It was a lovely day.

'There must be all of five thousand people

217

here,' said Hubert. 'Rather a shortage of lovely ladies, otherwise it might be Ascot or Aintree.'

'This is no time for gossip,' I said. 'Parade the cast.'

'But we don't open for another twenty minutes.'

'Jump to it,' I said. 'I'm going to address them. And Sergeant-Major—you can lock the outer door now. And give me the key.'

When the Gunners were assembled I said: 'I'm sure you're all going to do your best in this job. It's a bit out of the ordinary, but it's the gunner's boast that he can turn his hand to anything. There's one point, however, that some of you may not have thought of. You'll be handling quite a lot of money today. And there are bound to be nasty-minded people—particularly the ones who lose—who won't hesitate to start accusing you, and me, of fiddling their money. I have therefore taken steps to protect our reputations. In the far corner over there, the Sergeant-Major has a labelled sandbag for each of you. Write your name on the label so you'll know which one is yours. You will now empty everything out of your pockets into your own sandbag and hang the sandbag on one of those hooks on the back wall. They'll be under guard. Then, when the races are over, I've arranged for the provost to search all of you—and me. That will afford a complete answer to any accusations.'

I tried not to catch Gunner Whitehair's eye.

Ten minutes later the Tote was open. I can give you no very connected account of the afternoon. We moved from crisis to crisis.

There was the moment when I calculated the odds on the first winner, and they came to thirty-three to one. Hubert had the same answer. We dried the sweat from our foreheads and paid out. (There was no run on the Bank. Evidently this was an outsider.) There was the moment when the Brigadier insisted on a Double and wouldn't take no for an answer. All Totes had doubles. Why not ours? I deputed Hubert to deal with this one personally. Luckily both horses lost. There was the chronic difficulty with punters who staked in marks, lire, pounds (ordinary) and British Military currency, sometimes all in the same bet. There was the punter who tried to stake an Opel car which didn't belong to him; and the bad moment when we had to deal with a dead heat in the fifth race.

But all the time I had a feeling that this particular battle had been won before it started.

Three hours later, and feeling ten years older, I counted up the ten per cent take.

It was in small notes, and seemed to add up to just over two thousand pounds. It exactly filled a twenty-five pounder shell case.

As we were leaving, Gunner Whitehair

(who was a very friendly character) said to me: 'Went all right, didn't it, sir?'

'Like a dream,' I said.

'I believe we're going to have another next week.'

'Excellent,' I said.

'What you were saying about our characters, sir. It was all right this time, but supposing next time some of the boys have friends ready in the crowd, and just hand the lolly out to them through the window?'

'That will be Captain Featherstone's worry,' I said, 'not mine.'

CHURCHILL'S MEN

(<u>MUSIC UP. HELD UNDER</u>:-)

ANNOUNCER: Mr Behrens and Mr Calder belong to a very secret organisation headed by Fortescue—an organisation even more secret, and apparently more deadly than the celebrated M.I.5. Number Sixteen: 'CHURCHILL'S MEN'.

FORTESCUE: Ah, come in, Calder. Thank you MacKenzie.

(<u>DOOR SHUTS</u>)

FORTESCUE: Do you read war books?

CALDER: Only when they're about the Peninsular War.

FORTESCUE: Well, here's one about the last war. It's only in proof at the moment. The Cabinet Office decided to let me see it. In case there was a security angle—a very fortunate decision, as it turned out.

CALDER: (<u>Reading</u>) "Stormy Petrel".

221

Some passages in the life of a soldier and politician. By Captain Colin Mandeville D.S.C. (and bar).

FORTESCUE: You knew him in North Africa, I believe.

CALDER: I knew of him. Mercifully I was never in the same outfit.

FORTESCUE: And why do you say that?

CALDER: He was known to other officers in his regiment as Bubble Mandeville. On account of the fact that he was always seeking 'the bubble reputation, even in the cannon's mouth'. The trouble was, he usually wrote off all the chaps who were with him, and got away with it himself.

FORTESCUE: Not in the end. Not entirely.

CALDER: He lost an arm, if that's what you mean. And picked up two D.S.O.'s. Not a bad swap.

FORTESCUE: It would appear from this book that his gallantry appealed to Whitehall and when he left hospital he was given a junior ministerial job in the War Office, where he was concerned with Intelligence work.

CALDER: Then, thank goodness he never

222

controlled me. He'd no more brains than a bee.

FORTESCUE: That fact *was* appreciated, in time. His activities were confined to the basic training of agents. I've marked the place—in Chapter 5—there—

CALDER: Good heavens—

FORTESCUE: You see?

CALDER: That's absolutely crazy.

FORTESCUE: It'll have to come out of course. All those names must be deleted.

CALDER: I suppose we *can* make him—?

FORTESCUE: Most certainly we can. We have powers under the Official Secrets Act to have the whole book destroyed. But we don't want to do that. Apart from the names it's harmless enough. I'd like you to see him, and explain to him, gently but firmly, that these names must be omitted.

CALDER: Why don't you just write and tell him to cut them out?

FORTESCUE: Because Captain Mandeville is a troublemaker. I am not sufficiently expert, as an ornithologist, to know whether the stormy petrel was thought by the ancients to cause storms, or merely to herald their

223

	arrival. In Mandeville's case, both would be true.
CALDER:	In fact, an awkward customer—
FORTESCUE:	Yes, but with it all, he's not a bad person at heart. I'm sure that if the matter was put to him tactfully, we should have no trouble at all. May I leave it with you?

(<u>FADE OUT ON THIS</u>:-)

(<u>FADE IN ON</u>:-)

CAPT. MANDEVILLE:	Calder? Calder? You were in Four Commando you say?
CALDER:	For a few months.
CAPT. MANDEVILLE:	I can't pretend to remember your name, but I remember the unit, of course. Splendid bunch of chaps. Wasted as ordinary infantry. But we had to use what we had. And now you work for C.S.I. (E.). C.S.I. (E.)? That's old Fortescue's outfit isn't it?
CALDER:	That's right, Sir.
CAPT. MANDEVILLE:	Well now—?
CALDER:	It's rather a delicate matter. So Mr Fortescue thought I'd better explain it to you in

person. It makes it a lot easier that you were once involved in Intelligence yourself, so you know the form.

CAPT. MANDEVILLE: Once in the club, always of the club.

CALDER: Exactly. In Chapter Five of your book—which I've read, and much enjoyed, incidentally—you mention by name eight men and two women who passed through your Basic Intelligence Course. You pick them out as people who were outstanding, in one way or another.

CAPT. MANDEVILLE: Quite so.

CALDER: Five of them are dead, so it doesn't matter about them. But of the other five, three might possibly be useful to the Department again—I don't say they would be, but their special knowledge *might* be useful.

CAPT. MANDEVILLE: Yes. I see.

CALDER: The other two are Koba in Greece and—*most* particularly—Kyril Suzman in Poland.

CAPT. MANDEVILLE: Good heavens! I'd no idea. Are they still working for us? Suzman! Are you sure?

CALDER: Quite sure. He's the most valuable double in the whole organisation. I should add that only six men know it, and you're the seventh. If the other side got so much as a hint that Suzman had ever been trained in our Intelligence Schools—

CAPT. MANDEVILLE: My dear fellow. Don't say another word. Of course the names shall come out. *All* of them. *At* once. And you have my word that I'll forget what you've just told me. Suzman. Good God! Who'd have thought it—

(<u>FADE OUT</u>:-)

(<u>FADE IN ON</u>:-)

CALDER: Mandeville took it like a lamb.

FORTESCUE: I thought he would be reasonable if he was handled rightly. Have you read the book?

CALDER: I couldn't put it down. It ought to be called, 'How Churchill and I won the War'.

BEHRENS: *Not* Churchill and I. I and Churchill.

FORTESCUE: You have read the book, too, Behrens?

226

BEHRENS:	Indeed, yes.
FORTESCUE:	And what did you think of it?
BEHRENS:	I'm afraid my conclusion was that however much money Mandeville made out of it, he was bound to come out on the wrong side of the ledger at the end of the day.
FORTESCUE:	You think there'll be actions for libel?
BEHRENS:	Civil libel. Criminal libel. Slander of Title. Every action you can think of. In the old days he'd have been horse-whipped on the steps of the Naval and Military Club.
FORTESCUE:	I felt that some of his remarks were a mite injudicious.
BEHRENS:	And there's one man in particular who'll be after his scalp. The Right Honourable George Rybould.
FORTESCUE:	Politicians don't often sue for libel.
BEHRENS:	This politician will. I know George Rybould quite well—or did, before he rose to his present dizzy height in the Cabinet. He's a cold-blooded fish. In most matters his head rules his heart. But he's not going to pass this up.

(LEAVES BEING TURNED)

BEHRENS: Listen. This is September 1939. (Reads) In Whitehall I met George Rybould. He had just finished a spell as lecturer at the London School of Economics. I said to him, 'Well George, I imagine you'll be happy to get out of the classroom and into uniform. Which of the services have *you* picked on?' He said (book page turned) 'I haven't made up my mind yet. I thought of the Navy'. It was a month later, when I was in France with my Yeomanry Squadron, that I saw in the papers that he'd joined the Ministry of Information. Seeing that he was twenty-eight, and fit as a fiddle, I could only conclude that in his case discretion had proved to be very much the better part of valour. I fear I was angry enough to send him a note 'Congratulations on joining the H.M.S. M.O.I. I imagine she flies the yellow ensign'.

FORTESCUE: Hmmm.

228

CALDER:	He's not going to like *that.*
FORTESCUE:	But do you think he'll sue?
CALDER:	I'm certain he will. There are three things you must *never* say about a man. That he's hopeless in bed, that he can't drive a car, or that his physical courage is suspect.
BEHRENS:	It's particularly unfortunate in George Rybould's case. He was brought up by a doting mother, who was convinced he was delicate, and wouldn't let him go to boarding school. He had a tutor, and was in and out of one or two day schools.
FORTESCUE:	Why should that make any difference?
BEHRENS:	Foreigners have never understood our boarding school system. They call it barbaric. But there *was* a certain logic behind it. It grew up at a time when we had military and imperial commitments and it was thought to be appropriate training for these, for a boy to be savagely beaten and forced to take part in rough sports which could end in bruising and broken bones.

229

CALDER:	It toughened him up.
BEHRENS:	That was incidental. Indeed, I doubt whether you can 'toughen' a human being. He's not a piece of leather. No, the great advantage was that it showed a boy, at an early age, whether he had the faculty of supporting pain and discomfort or not. Some have, some haven't.
FORTESCUE:	(<u>At his most pawky</u>) Are you asserting, Behrens, that if a boy does not attend one of these barbaric establishments, *and* has the misfortune to grow up without being severely bruised or fracturing a limb—*and* the further misfortune to have no opportunity of being killed or maimed in warfare, that he will therefore be likely to be a physical coward?
BEHRENS:	Certainly not. The point is that he won't *know* whether he is a coward or not. He may suspect that he is. Now if that's the case with Rybould you can see why an accusation like this is going to catch him on the raw.
FORTESCUE:	Hm. It's an interesting speculation.

230

<u>(FADE OUT:-)</u>

<u>(FADE IN ON:-)</u>

MR BLAYDON Q.C.: Members of the Jury, it is not my intention to open the plaintiff's case to you at any great length. I need not tell you that the Right Honourable George Rybould has deserved well of his country. He has occupied, in succession, a number of responsible posts, at governmental, and now at Cabinet level. At present he is a Minister without portfolio, or, as he calls it, maid-of-all-work in the Cabinet and, if certain press predictions can be accepted as reliable, may very possibly attain shortly to the highest post of all. (<u>Pause for a sip of water</u>) It is fashionable, nowadays, to denigrate all politicians. I think, myself, that this is a mistake. By and large it is done simply because, being public figures, it is open to anyone who defames them to plead the defence known as 'fair comment'. This is a matter

231

which his Lordship will explain to you very fully, and therefore I will only touch on it. But what it means, in plain words, is that if you take part in public affairs you must expect people to talk about you. It is the price you pay for being a public figure. And the law says—and it is perfectly logical—that whilst a private person can object to having his private life, his private strengths—and weaknesses—exposed to the world, a *public* person does not enjoy this advantage. In short, if he puts himself on the stage, he cannot complain of the limelight. (Second pause for a sip) *But*, members of the Jury, there is one exception to this rule. The defence is one of *fair* comment. If it can be shown that the comment is *un*fair—particularly if it can be shown to have been motivated by malice—(Mr Blaydon pauses a moment to allow the word to echo round the Court)—malice, or spite, then the situation is very different. In such circumstances your public man has as much right to the protection of this Court as anyone else. It will be my duty—an unpleasant duty—to call before you a number of eminent witnesses, whose evidence in some cases goes back to the days of the War and who will, I submit, be able to show that the defendant, Mandeville, has quarrelled more than once with the plaintiff, and, as a result of these differences of opinion, has pursued a deliberate and systematic campaign of denigration. That is all I have to say to you for the moment and I will therefore—

JUDGE: Mr Blaydon.

MR BLAYDON Q.C.: My Lord?

JUDGE: I observe that it is now five minutes to one. Would this not be a convenient moment to adjourn? That will enable your witnesses to fortify themselves with a good luncheon before they are called.

MR BLAYDON Q.C.: A most humane suggestion, my Lord.

USHER: The Court will rise—

(FADE OUT:- ON
MURMURS ETC.)

(FADE IN ON:-)

BEHRENS:	I'm not at all happy about the way things are going, sir.
FORTESCUE:	Oh, why, Behrens?
BEHRENS:	It looks as if Rybould intends to rake up a lot of dirt about his wartime bickering with Mandeville. If he does that, we'll be back to square one. Names will be flung about all over the place.
FORTESCUE:	Yes. I see.
BEHRENS:	The case is getting a lot of news coverage as it is. After Counsel's broad hint this morning that he'd got a few bombs to explode this afternoon, it's going to be front page, headline stuff, and no mistake.
FORTESCUE:	I'll have the Attorney General alerted. If anything undesirable seems to be developing he will have to intervene on grounds of public interest.
BEHRENS:	Do you think that will be effective?
FORTESCUE:	Frankly, Behrens, no. I don't.

234

	But it's the best I can think of at the moment. The only really safe course would be to stop the case altogether.
BEHRENS:	We've got one thing in our favour. It's Friday today, and the Court doesn't sit on Saturdays. I gather that the first part of the afternoon will be taken up with formal evidence. Proof of the publication, and so on. With any luck we shan't reach the dangerous stuff before the Court recesses at four o'clock.
FORTESCUE:	Let us hope you are right.

(<u>FADE OUT</u>:-)

(<u>COME IN ON THE MURMUR OF A PACKED COURT ROOM. THIS IS STILLED AS MR BLAYDON RISES TO HIS FEET AFTER THE CROSS-EXAMINATION OF HIS LAST FORMAL WITNESS</u>)

| MR BLAYDON Q.C.: | I will now call the plaintiff in this case, The Right Honourable George Rybould. |

235

(THE TAKING OF THE
OATH BY RYBOULD IN
TRADITIONAL FORM IS
HEARD AS A
BACKGROUND
ACCOMPANIMENT TO:-)

BEHRENS: (<u>Sotto voce</u>) Three forty-five. Pipped at the post.

CALDER: (<u>Sotto voce</u>) That publisher let us down. He was too bloody quick.

BEHRENS: The Attorney General doesn't look too happy.

CALDER: What can he do?

BEHRENS: Ask for the Court to be cleared, I suppose.

(BRING UP THE
WITNESS'S VOICE FROM
BACKGROUND TO
FOREGROUND)

MR BLAYDON Q.C.: Your name is George Patrick Rybould, you are a Companion of Honour, a member of the Privy Council and a Member of Parliament?

RYBOULD: (<u>An incisive speaker</u>) That is correct.

MR BLAYDON Q.C.: I should like to draw your attention straight away to the passage in the book, entitled

236

'Stormy Petrel', which as the Jury have heard, from witnesses already called, was written by the defendant, Captain Mandeville, and published for him by his co-defendants in this case, Finemore Press Limited. I need not read it to you again. But would like you to tell the Jury, quite simply, what you took it to mean.

RYBOULD: I took it to mean that I was a coward.

MR BLAYDON Q.C.: That was how you read it. And that, to the best of your knowledge, was how your friends read it?

RYBOULD: Naturally. It was a plain accusation, and made in the most offensive manner possible.

MR BLAYDON Q.C. In fact, the accusation was originally made in a private letter to you, was it not?

RYBOULD: That is correct.

MR BLAYDON Q.C. What did you do with the letter?

RYBOULD: I tore it up.

MR BLAYDON Q.C. So that, in its original form, it received no publicity at all?

RYBOULD: No.

MR BLAYDON Q.C. But now it has been reported

	with the maximum possible publicity. And that is the gravamen of your complaint?
RYBOULD:	Right.
MR BLAYDON Q.C.	Now, Mr Rybould, I had better ask you this question, because if I don't I'm perfectly certain that my learned friend will. In September 1939 you were suffering from no medical disability?
RYBOULD:	I was perfectly fit.
MR BLAYDON Q.C.	And you were not in a reserved occupation?
RYBOULD:	No.
MR BLAYDON Q.C.	Then why did you join the Ministry of Information in preference to the Army, the Navy or the Air Force?
RYBOULD:	Because I was sure that I should have been quite useless in the Services. But I thought I might be reasonably effective as a propagandist.
MR BLAYDON Q.C.	Looking back on your decision, do you think it was a correct one?
RYBOULD:	I thought so then, and I think so now.
MR BLAYDON Q.C.	Indeed, judging by results, it proved so, did it not—perhaps, My Lord, I can lead on this:

238

	after a sojourn with Overseas Broadcasting in 1940 and 1941 you were transferred to the Foreign Office, on attachment, where you worked for the rest of the war?
RYBOULD:	That's correct.
MR BLAYDON Q.C.	Would you explain to the Jury exactly what the Department, which you set up in the Foreign Office, dealt with?
RYBOULD:	(<u>Loudly</u>) In 1944—
MR BLAYDON Q.C.	To the Jury please.
RYBOULD:	(<u>Turning away—but still perfectly audible</u>) In 1944, when it became apparent that Germany was going to be defeated, I was charged with the training, and, if you like, indoctrination of various nationals who had come over to England, and were politically prominent in their own countries, with the idea of affording them facilities for returning to those countries as quickly as opportunity offered. The idea was that at the moment the Germans drew out, leaving a political vacuum behind them, these people could set up, or help to set up,

	a government friendly to this country.
MR BLAYDON Q.C.	And was the defendant, Captain Mandeville, concerned with your department?
RYBOULD:	He was the Junior Minister, with a general supervision over it; and other departments.
MR BLAYDON Q.C.	Did you gather whether he approved of the project you have just explained to us?
RYBOULD:	I gathered that he did *not* approve of it.
MR BLAYDON Q.C.	On what grounds?
RYBOULD:	Generally, because he thought wars should be fought by soldiers, not by politicians. In particular because he thought it represented a security risk to send men who had passed the last five years in England, in positions of confidence, back, as he put it, 'into the arms of the Russians'.
MR BLAYDON Q.C.:	And did this cause friction between you?
RYBOULD:	There were a number of most disagreeable exchanges. But the matter came to a head when—(he is just about to mention Suzman's name).
ATTORNEY GENERAL:	My Lord.

240

JUDGE:	Yes, Mr Attorney General.
ATTORNEY GENERAL:	My Lord, I am here in my official capacity as representing the Crown. There is a submission which I shall have to make to your Lordship, but I am in some difficulty.
JUDGE:	Proceed.
ATTORNEY GENERAL:	I was only instructed in this matter at ten minutes to two this afternoon. And my instructions raise matters of considerable complexity. I therefore—
JUDGE:	I may be able to help you. I observe that the time is five minutes to four. What I shall do is to adjourn now. That will give you until ten o'clock on Monday to take full instructions and make your submission in whatever form you see fit.
ATTORNEY GENERAL:	I am much obliged.
USHER:	The Court will rise—

(FADE OUT ON THIS:-)

(FADE IN ON:-)

CALDER:	Saved by the bell!
BEHRENS:	I must confess I was sweating. I

241

thought the Attorney General had left it too late. Then the Judge, bless him, called time.

FORTESCUE: You think that Rybould was on the point of mentioning Suzman's name?

CALDER: I'm damned sure he was. That was the cause of the big row. You know what happened. As soon as Suzman reached Warsaw, he went over lock, stock and barrel, to the Russians. A very small circle of people—not more than half a dozen here and in America—knew that this was part of the overall plan.

BEHRENS: And that half dozen did *not* include Captain Mandeville, I assume?

CALDER: Tell Mandeville! You might just as well have told the town crier.

BEHRENS: Nor Rybould?

CALDER: No. Not Rybould either. As far as he was concerned, it was part of his ordinary job. Grooming pro-allied politicians for central Europe.

BEHRENS: I see. So when the Suzman project turned sour—or appeared to do so—both of

242

	them were in a position to blame each other.
CALDER:	That's right. Rybould, like most politicians, knows very little about Intelligence work, and doesn't like what he does know. His line was, if you M.I.6. people monkey about with my men, you must expect them to double-cross you. Mandeville, of course, took the opposite view. He said, once a man has been coached by M.I.6. and given access to all sorts of top secret details, it's madness to put him back into the hands of the enemy.
BEHRENS:	Did any of this get out?
CALDER:	Judging by results, no. If the Russians had thought for a moment that Suzman had ever been connected with M.I.6., they would never have allowed him to attain the position he has.
CALDER:	The only position he'd have attained would have been a horizontal one, in a six foot trench. And *that's* still possible.
BEHRENS:	Couldn't we have the public turned out and the case continued in closed court?

243

FORTESCUE:	That is what the Attorney General was instructed to ask for. And it's what he will ask for on Monday, if he has to. But I'm not convinced that it's effective.
CALDER:	It certainly wasn't in the Blake case.
FORTESCUE:	The press and the general public are excluded. But there are still far too many people to guard a top level secret. The barristers, the solicitors, the solicitors' clerks, the court officials, the short-hand writers—none of these people are subject to any security precautions at all.
BEHRENS:	That's true enough. I'm sure I could walk into my own solicitor's office in the lunch hour and purloin any paper I wanted.
CALDER:	Besides, by asking for the Court to be cleared we draw attention to the precise point we want to keep under hatches.
BEHRENS:	If that's right, we're on to a beating either way. Continue in open Court and we tell the world. Clear the Court, and we start people thinking.

FORTESCUE:	There *is* a solution. Rybould must be persuaded to drop the case. Then it would only be necessary to announce on Monday that it had been settled on agreed terms. And it would attract no attention at all.
BEHRENS:	I know George Rybould fairly well. And I can assure you that he's not an easy man to persuade.
FORTESCUE:	Quite so. And since you know him, you are going to do the persuading.
BEHRENS:	I had a feeling you might be going to say that.

(FADE OUT ON BEHRENS:-)

(FADE IN ON BIG BEN, AT A DISTANCE, CHIMING THE HALF HOUR. WE ARE IN A PRIVATE ROOM IN THE HOUSES OF PARLIAMENT)

RYBOULD:	(The slight pause before he speaks suggests that he has been giving thought to the plea put to him by Behrens) Mm. I

appreciate your frankness in telling me this, Behrens, and I need hardly say that I will treat the — (_h e s i t a t e s_) — the background information as entirely and completely confidential. But I can't go any further than that.

BEHRENS: You mean that you still propose to produce, in Court, the details of your quarrel with Captain Mandeville?

RYBOULD: In closed Court, if necessary.

BEHRENS: In spite of the inevitable risks of a leak?

RYBOULD: I don't regard the risks as inevitable.

BEHRENS: Well, we'll agree to differ about that. I appreciate that if you're to demonstrate malice, you've got to give some details of the bad blood between the two of you. But don't you think you could do it in a more general way? Just say that there were differences of opinion over the handling of A, B and C—not giving names and details—

RYBOULD: I considered such a course, but I was advised, by Leading Counsel, that it would be quite impractical. If we are to make

246

	our case, we must make it fully, with details. Otherwise it will be laughed out of Court.
BEHRENS:	Yes. I see that difficulty. All the same—
RYBOULD:	(<u>Overriding him</u>) And another thing. You talk about a security risk. I don't want to be rude about this, but I sometimes think that the trouble with all you Intelligence people is that you live in the past. You still see spies and enemy agents lurking in every shadow. Like a revered aunt of mine who is *convinced* that there is a burglar under every bed she occupies!
BEHRENS:	You're not suggesting that the great powers have dismantled their Intelligence machines, are you, because if you are—
RYBOULD:	No, no. I'm not saying that at all. If anything they're bigger than they were. But they use different methods, now, Behrens. Kidnapping and murder are out of fashion. It's all overflight and photography and propaganda worked out on giant computers. There's not a lot of difference nowadays

between an Intelligence organisation and an advertising agency. They need facts. And research to produce facts. But basically they're out to capture men's minds.

BEHRENS: I think you're over-simplifying the problem, Minister.

RYBOULD: Well, we won't quarrel about it. You shall have your secret session, and I'll have another word with Counsel to see if we can't soften down some of the details. Will that satisfy you?

BEHRENS: We haven't got a lot of time, you know.

RYBOULD: True. Wait a moment whilst I look at my diary. I've got a meeting in Birmingham tomorrow morning. Lunch with the constituency officers. And I'm supposed to be opening a fete during the afternoon—who says politicians don't earn their salaries? I could probably get Blaydon over some time early Saturday evening—he lives not far from me. Look here! Why not come down and spend Saturday night? It's a quiet place, but I can give you simple bachelor comfort.

	Including some drinkable port.
BEHRENS:	Well—
RYBOULD:	If you refuse, I shall conclude that you're seriously annoyed with me. And I should be sorry about that.
BEHRENS:	If you put it that way, I can hardly refuse. The port seems to me to be a clinching argument—

(<u>FADE OUT ON THIS</u>:-)

(<u>FADE IN ON</u>:-)

BEHRENS:	Dammit, that fellow Rybould has certainly got the gift of the gab. He hadn't been talking to me for five minutes before I began to wonder whether he wasn't right, and we weren't being quite unreasonable.
FORTESCUE:	He has asked you down for the weekend?
BEHRENS:	Yes. His Counsel, Mr Blaydon Q.C., lives in the neighbourhood and is coming across after tea to discuss whether we can't keep things on a Mr A Mr B basis. I've a feeling he won't agree.
FORTESCUE:	Do you think it's wise?

BEHRENS:	Is what wise?
FORTESCUE:	Your going to stay with him. You realise that he may be under observation.
BEHRENS:	Do you think so?
FORTESCUE:	Perhaps not.
BEHRENS:	And if they *do* think there's anything behind it, they're just as likely to assume that I've been posted down there to protect Rybould from their attention.
FORTESCUE:	That possibility had not occurred to me. It is, of course, a fairly lonely house, in its own grounds, and about half a mile from the village. Yes. (<u>Pause</u>) Yes. I had been going to suggest that you should conceal your arrival, but I've changed my mind. I think, in all the circumstances, it would be better for you to go down quite openly—

(<u>FADE OUT</u>:-)

(<u>FADE IN ON</u>:-)

RYBOULD:	Now fill up your glass Behrens and push the decanter along.

(SOUND OF DECANTER AND GLASSES)

BEHRENS:	Thank you. I'm afraid we didn't have much success with Mr Blaydon.
RYBOULD:	I warned you. You know what these lawyers are, once they get their teeth into a case.
BEHRENS:	Apparently he not only insists on dragging out the full details of the Suzman affair—but now he wants to subpoena at least one—possibly two—retired officials from the Foreign Office to give evidence.
RYBOULD:	One of them will be old Masterman. They'll certainly have to clear the Court if they put *him* in the box. (Chuckles)
BEHRENS:	(Not responding) Yes. (Pause) Look here. I don't want to abuse your hospitality in any way, and I certainly didn't come down here to argue with you, but, as I told you, we've no great confidence in the security of closed court proceedings.
RYBOULD:	You may be right about that. I wouldn't know.
BEHRENS:	I suppose I couldn't persuade you, even at this late hour, to drop the whole thing, could I?

251

<u>(A PAUSE)</u>

RYBOULD: No. I'm afraid you couldn't. I recognise the argument of the public good. I think you've put it very fairly. I just don't happen to consider that the risks are as real as you seem to think they are. I've stood a great deal from Mandeville in the past. This time he's gone too far.

BEHRENS: Well—I had to try. I think I'll turn in. Are you coming?

RYBOULD: Alas, I've got a full hours work to do with these papers.

BEHRENS: They make you work for your living.

RYBOULD: They do that. You can find your own way up?

BEHRENS: Surely. Good night.

RYBOULD: Good night.

<u>(DOOR OPENS AND SHUTS)</u>

<u>(RYBOULD GETTING UP AND SWITCHING ON RADIO)</u>

NEWS ANNOUNCER: '—Road accident figures, which are once again on the increase. Fatal accidents, an increase of fifteen per cent in the last quarter. Serious injuries an increase of seventeen per cent. (<u>Pause</u>) The first day of the hearing of the action for libel by the Right Honourable George Rybould against Captain Mandeville opened in the Queen's Bench Division of the High Court today. A number of witnesses from Government Departments are to be called on to give evidence. It is anticipated that the Attorney General will apply on Monday morning to have the Court cleared—

(<u>BEHIND THIS, A SOUND OF MOVEMENT. AS THE LATCH OF THE CURTAINED FRENCH WINDOW IS FORCED, MAKING RATHER MORE NOISE THAN THE INTRUDER INTENDED</u>)

(<u>SLIGHT SOUND OF WIND AS FRENCH WINDOWS OPEN</u>)

253

RYBOULD: (Switching off the set) Hullo! Who's that? (Pause)

(FRENCH WINDOWS SHUT WITH CLICK. CUT WIND)

RYBOULD: Who the devil are you?

INTRUDER (CALDER): (He speaks with a slight foreign accent) (Rather slowly) That is a singularly stupid question. Do you imagine that I am going to hand you my visiting card, with my name and address engraved on it?

RYBOULD: What—what do you want?

INTRUDER (CALDER): Sit down.

(WHEN RYBOULD DOESN'T MOVE, HE REPEATS THIS, MUCH MORE SHARPLY)

INTRUDER (CALDER): Sit down. I think we had better get one or two things clear to start with. The weapon I have here is a cyanide gun. It is extremely powerful, and quite silent. If I have to do so, I shall shoot you in the face with it, and you will die in thirty seconds. But they will not be a pleasant thirty seconds. By the

254

end of it, you will probably be glad to die. Do you understand *that*?

RYBOULD: (<u>Sotto voce</u>) I understand.

INTRUDER (CALDER): The second thing is that when I ask you a question, I require it to be answered, at once, and without prevarication. If you do not, I shall hurt you. There are a number of ways in which I can do that. Some are more painful than others. Since time is short, I shall choose the most painful.

RYBOULD: What do you want me to tell you?

INTRUDER (CALDER): It is very simple. You are engaged in a law suit. It has reached the point at which you were about to describe the Intelligence training of certain foreigners who came to England during the war. Is that right?

RYBOULD: Well—aah.

INTRUDER (CALDER): That was only your foot. No bones broken. Next time it will be your knee. That may not be so comfortable. Now I will repeat the question. You were about to name certain foreigners who passed through

255

your hands. Right?

RYBOULD: (<u>As before</u>) Yes.

INTRUDER (CALDER): Then, Mr Rybould, instead of speaking them in Court, you will speak them to me—now—in private. Yes?

RYBOULD: (<u>Pause</u>) No.

INTRUDER (CALDER): Think hard before you refuse, Mr Rybould. You will have to speak in the end.

RYBOULD: No.

INTRUDER (CALDER): Very well. Remove your right shoe.

(<u>A VICIOUS THUD, FOLLOWED BY A GASP OF PAIN FROM RYBOULD</u>)

INTRUDER (CALDER): Remove your right shoe. (<u>Pause</u>) And your sock. Now, Mr Rybould, unless you do what I say, I will hold your foot on the electric fire for ten seconds. I assure you, I am quite capable of doing it, even if I have to cripple you first. Well—? (<u>Pause</u>) Well, Mr Rybould.

RYBOULD: (<u>Low, but quite clear</u>) You can do what you like, I'm not going to tell you.

256

(SIMULTANEOUSLY, A
FURTHER BLOW. FEET
RUNNING IN THE
PASSAGE. THE SOUND OF
THE INTRUDER
DEPARTING THROUGH
THE OPEN FRENCH
WINDOW. FOLLOWED BY
THE DOOR BURSTING
OPEN.)

BEHRENS: Rybould! What's up, man? I heard the noise—
RYBOULD: Man—through the window—
BEHRENS: Where's the telephone?

(SOUND OF RECEIVER
BEING TAKEN OFF AND
'JIGGLED')

BEHRENS: No good. He's probably cut the wire.
RYBOULD: Watch out. He's got a gun.
BEHRENS: So have I.

(PAUSE)

BEHRENS: He's away. I'll have to use my car to get to a telephone that works. I'll leave you the gun. Have you ever used one?
RYBOULD: No.

257

BEHRENS:	It isn't difficult. You point it and pull the trigger.
RYBOULD:	All right. Behrens—
BEHRENS:	(<u>At door</u>) Yes?
RYBOULD:	I didn't tell him anything.

(<u>FADE OUT</u>:-)

(<u>FADE IN ON</u>:-)

ANNOUNCER:	Counsel for the Right Honourable George Rybould informed the Court this morning that the parties had been able to agree terms of settlement. It was agreed that certain passages would be deleted in future editions of the book. Mr Justice Mainwaring therefore ordered the record to be expunged. It is believed that other parties are considering action in connection with other passages in the book—

(<u>FADE OUT</u>:-)

(<u>FADE IN ON</u>:-)

FORTESCUE:	I understand that the initiatve for settling the action came

from Rybould himself. Is that true, Behrens?

BEHRENS: That's true. Rybould got off his high horse and went along to see Mandeville and put it to him—couldn't they settle the matter sensibly between them. Mandeville isn't a bad chap really—and he was pretty tired of it, too. Nobody really enjoys litigation—except the lawyers. So he said, O.K. and they shook on it.

FORTESCUE: And what do you suppose can have caused such an extraordinary change of heart in Rybould?

BEHRENS: Oh, a lot of things. First, after what happened to him on Friday night he wasn't prepared to write off M.I.6. as a lot of scaremongers. Then, quite a lot of people, whose opinion mattered to him, know that he really is a man of courage. But the most important thing of all is that he now knows it himself. So he doesn't have to go round proving it.

FORTESCUE: I see. Yes. Very satisfactory. Very satisfactory. By the way.

Did Rybould know Calder?

BEHRENS: (<u>Taken off guard</u>) Er—No, I don't think he did.

FORTESCUE: And where was Calder on Friday night?

BEHRENS: Why? Has someone been enquiring after him?

FORTESCUE: In the course of their routine investigations it was reported to the local Police—by some youth, who was out late that night—courting, I don't doubt—that he had observed an old Austin two-seater, with an open dicky-seat. It was partly concealed in some bushes near Rybould's house. Calder has an old Austin two-seater hasn't he?

BEHRENS: Yes. But so have a lot of people. (<u>Casually</u>) Did the boy happen to notice the number?

FORTESCUE: No. But he did happen to observe a very large dog, seated in the dicky. He thought it was a deer-hound, but couldn't be sure.

BEHRENS: I see.

FORTESCUE: There's just one thing about this that puzzles me. (<u>Pause</u>) How did you know when to burst in?

260

BEHRENS:	Oh, I was listening outside the door.
FORTESCUE:	And if Rybould <u>hadn't</u> spoken up, as soon as he did, would you have allowed Calder to burn his feet in the electric fire.
BEHRENS:	Perhaps just a little.
FORTESCUE:	Wasn't that—rather—unethical?
BEHRENS:	I was thinking of what the Russians would have done to Suzman if they'd suspected him.
FORTESCUE:	Mphm.

(<u>MUSIC. UP AND OUT</u>)

CORONATION YEAR

'Went off nice, didn't it?' said Mr Burger, removing his billycock hat and placing it carefully on the bar counter.

'Not what you'd call a hot day, not for June,' said Mr Jopling. 'All the better for that perhaps.'

'You don't want a very hot day,' agreed Mr Burger. 'Not with all them crowds.'

'We had a fizzer when they did Teddy. Ten years ago, wasn't it?'

'Nine,' said Mr Jopling.

'Nine. That's right. Thermometer in the eighties. Women fainting. Remember?'

'Certainly I remember *that* occasion,' said Mr Burger bitterly. 'A dozen of us clubbed together to hire an upstairs room in the Strand. And what happened? It got itself put off. Three pounds a head that cost us.'

'I don't see you can blame Teddy for that. He couldn't help having appendicitis. Might have happened to anyone.'

'So it might,' agreed Mr Burger. 'All I'm saying is, I wasn't risking anything like that this time. Went down early and found myself a place on the pavement in Piccadilly. Got a good view of them driving back from the Abbey. Very nice they looked, too.'

'A handsome pair,' agreed Mr Stoop. 'Now,

262

wottle-it-be?'

The invitation included Mr Jopling.

'The usual, thank you, Charlie,' said Mr Burger. Mr Jopling nodded his agreement.

'Three pints of old and mild, Jack,' said Mr Stoop, 'and have one for yourself.' He slammed down his shilling on the bar. It rang on the mahogany, a bright new shilling minted to celebrate a bright new reign.

'Some year, taken all round,' said Mr Burger. 'Coronation, Naval Review. Kids' tea party at the Crystal Palace. Now this march past. Someone has to pay for it all, I suppose.' He glanced out of the window at the sanded street, and the crowd that had already started to gather on the pavement.

'Year started well, too,' said Mr Stoop. 'Clapham Common and Sidney Street.'

This remark was felt to be in doubtful taste.

'I venture to think,' said Mr Jopling, who was tall and serious, and a student of affairs, 'that there are other things than two sordid outbreaks of crime for which this year of grace will be held memorable. In my view it will go down in history as the year in which the legislative power of the Upper House was first seriously challenged. If the debate goes the wrong way, we shall feel the effects of *that* for many a long year, mark my words.'

'I read in the papers,' said Mr Burger, 'that some Italians in Tripoli dropped a bomb out of an airplane.'

'What in the world did they do that for?' said Mr Stoop.

'I suppose they were aiming to kill someone.'

'Crazy,' said Mr Stoop. 'My nephew, he was out in South Africa for two years with the C.I.V., he told me it was difficult enough to hit a man with a bomb when you and him was both standing still. What chance would you have in an airplane?'

'True enough,' said Mr Burger. 'Look at that business in Madrid four years ago. All that chap had got to do was lob one out of an hotel window into a ruddy great coach and four. And then he went and missed.'

'Five,' said Mr Jopling.

Mr Stoop counted up on his fingers. 'That's right. Five years ago. Come to think of it, that was quite a year, too. Funny, isn't it, how some years everything seems to happen. Frisco earthquake. Typhoon in Hong Kong. Olympic Games.'

'Asquith's first budget,' said Mr Jopling, patiently raising the tone of the conversation.

'Hackenschmidt and Madrali at Olympia,' said Mr Stoop, lowering it again. 'Then take the year after. Dull as ditch-water.'

'Ah,' said Mr Burger. He finished his pint and placed his glass on the counter.

'South African cricketers. They were over that year.'

'Colonial Conference,' said Mr Jopling.

Neither was felt to be a matter of memorable importance.

'Ah,' said Mr Burger again. 'Some might think it a dull year. Not me though. It's a year I shan't forget in a hurry.'

'Cut your first tooth?' suggested Mr Stoop facetiously.

'That was the year I had lodger trouble.'

Silence descended on the trio. Mr Burger had spoken a word of power. He had the attention of the company.

'That was the year *that* happened, was it?' said Mr Stoop thoughtfully. 'So it was. I'd forgotten.'

'Very unfortunate business,' said Mr Jopling. A sense of the importance of world events seemed to be struggling with human curiosity. 'I never did hear what happened, really. Plenty of rumours.'

'After it was all over,' said Mr Burger, 'I promised my old lady I wouldn't talk about it. Now she's gone'—he touched the faded black band on his left sleeve—'and now that all that time's gone by, it really would be a sort of relief to talk about it.'

Mr Jopling motioned quietly to the landlord, who refilled their glasses, and then leaned his elbows on the bar so as not to miss a word. From outside, the shouts of the crowd came distantly and indistinctly.

'Lodgers,' said Mr Burger, 'are what I never really could get used to. They brought in money, but they brought in trouble, too. Trouble and hard work.'

Here Mr Burger knew, and Mr Burger's listeners knew, he did himself rather more than justice. His flat-fronted North London house had not been run by him. It had been run by his wife, Alice. In spite of her small size and meek look, Alice had been a running woman. She had run the house, the maid, and the lodgers, and she had also run Mr Burger, whose contribution to the common purse had consisted of important but unspecified work in the Caledonian Market. Yet despite all her running, she had contrived to remain an essentially feminine woman. This was one of the crosses that Mr Burger had had to bear.

The other cross was their maid, Tania.

'Speak no ill,' he said, 'but she was a difficult girl. Moody. Keep her busy and she was all right. Let her stop for a moment, and she fell into the dumps. Sit for half an hour at a time, in a chair, with her hands folded, thinking about God knows what.'

'I expect she was thinking about the foreign parts she came from,' said Mr Jopling.

'Or boys,' suggested Mr Stoop. 'Mostly when girls seem to be thinking about nothing they're thinking about boys.'

'Pretty?' asked the landlord.

'In a way.' Mr Burger spoke as a man to whom mere material prettiness meant nothing. 'The word I'd have used would be—

266

susceptible. And with Barker in the house it didn't do to have a susceptible girl around. I can see that now. He was a holy terror with girls, old Barker was. We called him old Barker, not that he was all that old, come to think of it. But he was getting to an age when a man begins to doubt his powers, and has to prove himself wrong every girl he meets.'

'Traveller, wasn't he?' said Mr Jopling.

'Soap. Travelled in soap. "I spend my life cleaning up the world," he used to say. Wouldn't have done any harm if he'd cleaned himself up a bit. Morally, I mean. He could do what he liked when he was on the road, but in my house he had to behave himself. I had to warn him more than once. Him and Alice. Duets. I soon put a stop to *that,* I can tell you.'

'I wonder you tolerated him in the house,' said Mr Jopling.

'So do I,' said Mr Burger. 'But it's easy to be wise after the event, isn't it? If I'd known what was going to happen I'd have got rid of him, of course. But a lodger who paid his bill regular was a thing you thought twice about losing. Even a man like Barker. And it wasn't only him carrying on with every bit of skirt he set eyes on. He'd a nasty tongue, too.'

'He liked an argument,' agreed Mr Stoop. 'I heard him in here more than once.'

'Argue?' said Mr Burger. 'He'd no more idea of arguing than my dog Toby. Just shout the other man down. The lodgers didn't like it above half. A quiet debate, that was one thing. But not a slanging match. We lost more than one lodger on account of Barker. In fact, at the time I'm talking about, we'd only two others with us. There was Mr Crocker, who was deaf and hardly ever came out of his room. And this young chap. A sort of foreigner, white face, black hair sticking up like a mop, and a small pointed beard, that made him look even younger than he was, somehow. Middle twenties, I'd have said. Came from somewhere over there.' Mr Burger waved his hand expansively in the direction of the Eastern hemisphere—'I called him Joe. His real name I never could get my tongue round.'

'Pole,' suggested Mr Jopling.

'Very likely. I can tell you one thing. He wasn't French. I tried him in French once, and he never understood a word I said. I did think, at one time, he might have come from the same parts as Tania. I heard them once, jabber-jabbering together in some foreign lingo. Not that he ever paid much attention to her. He was a serious sort of youngster. When he did say anything it was mostly economics and politics and such.'

Mr Jopling approved of that. 'I'd have liked to have met him,' he said.

'You'd have made a pair. He was over in England for a conference. Summer school, or something, at the Brotherhood Church Hall.

Out he'd go after breakfast, and back after tea. Talk all day to his compatriots, I don't doubt, but we never had a lot out of him when he got home.'

'He could talk English then,' said Mr Stoop.

'When he first arrived, it was just a few words. But he picked it up wonderful quick. I tell you, he'd a good head on him. By the time he'd been with us a month or so he was stringing sentences together. Quite interesting to listen to, some of his ideas. Then, in the middle of it, old Barker would blow in, half cut, and start taking the mickey out of him. "Some people," he'd say, "never done a hand's turn of real work in their lives. Nothing but talk. That's all you and your friends ever do, isn't it? You produce enough gas between you to fill a gas works." Or it might be, "My advice to you, Joe, is cut the cackle. And whilst you're about it, get your hair cut, too."'

'Tsk, tsk,' said Mr Jopling. 'That wasn't very polite. What did Joe say?'

'Nothing,' said Mr Burger. 'Nothing at all. I did wonder, sometimes, if he understood him. From what happened later, I think he must have done. Well, as I was telling you, it was about that time we had our trouble. It would have been—let me think—one night toward the end of May, I woke up, smelling gas. Alice said, "You're always smelling things. Go to sleep." I said, "I think I'll just make sure." So

I went down. Nothing downstairs. Then I came up again, and it was stronger. "Must be up in the attic," I thought. Only Tania slept up there. I went up, and found her door was locked. I thought, "She's gone to sleep and left her fire on, silly girl." As for locking the door, I didn't think anything of that. If I'd been a girl I'd have locked *my* door with Barker sleeping in the room below. I banged on the door. Nothing doing. Then I remembered you could get at the window from the roof. Sort of catwalk with a parapet to stop you slipping off. I hopped out and went along. The window was tight shut, but I broke that and got in and turned the gas fire out. Wasn't any use. I might just as well have stayed in bed for any good I could do. She was dead. Nearly passed out myself. I tried to get out of the door, but the key wasn't in the lock. Then I got back to the window, and, tell you the truth, I was sick. Then we got the police.'

Mr Burger took a pull of his beer to revive himself.

'Very nice, the police was. We had a Sergeant come round from the local station. His first idea was accident. Was she a careful sort of girl? Well, we had to say "No" to that. If anyone left a light on, or a tap running, it was pretty certain to be Tania. "Then perhaps," said the Sergeant, "she went to sleep with the fire on, and the draft blew it out."

'"Where comes the draft if the door was locked and the window shut?" says Joe, who'd been listening to me and the Sergeant.

'Well, that was a bit of a poser, but we didn't stick on it, because the next thing we got was the doctor's report, and that was that.'

'She was—?'

'Yes,' said Mr Burger. 'She was. Five months gone. Well, of course, that put a different complexion on things. A girl in that condition will do anything. And the more you looked at it, the more it did look like suicide. The window tight shut and latched, although it was a warm night. The door locked. There was only one key, as far as we knew, and that was under her pillow. What's more, there was a bottle of sleeping pills on the table by her bed. It was a new bottle, five or six gone. Not enough to hurt her, see, but enough to make her sleepy. Then she turns the gas on, gets into bed, and dozes off—'

'Sad,' said Mr Stoop. 'Sad. But a judgement really.'

'Ah,' said Mr Burger, 'but it didn't end there. Not by half. The next thing was we lost the cruets.'

'Cruets?'

'A week later. All the cruets out of the sideboard cupboard. Wedding presents, most of them. Solid silver. Alice was very put out. So we had the police in once more. It was the same Sergeant. "Well," he said, "troubles

271

never come singly. What's happened this time?" We were all there that evening, in the dining room. Even old Mr Crocker, not that he understood much of what was going on.

' "Anyone might have walked in and picked them up, I suppose," says Alice. "The front door's on the latch all day."

'The Sergeant looked as if he couldn't quite swallow this. It wasn't as if the house was left empty. It'd be pretty cool for a stranger to walk in and empty the sideboard.

' "Me, I think," says Joe, "it would be more natural to suspect one of us, yes?"

'Well, so did I, but no one had quite liked to say it.

' "Since I am a stranger, I should be most suspect. I insist that my room and luggage are searched."

'This cheered the Sergeant up a lot. It's what he'd wanted to do anyway. Then we explained it all to Mr Crocker, who nearly busted himself laughing, and said, come along, they could search his luggage, and him too if they wanted to. Old Barker looked very put out, but of course he had to go along with the others. After all, it would have looked pretty funny if he hadn't, wouldn't it?'

'And did he find the cruets?' said Mr Stoop.

'No,' said Mr Burger, pausing to take a couple of inches off his drink. 'He didn't find the cruets. But he found a key, at the bottom of old Barker's suitcase, tucked away under a pile of shirts, a bright, new, shiny duplicate of the key to Tania's bedroom. It didn't take the Sergeant long to work *that* out. Not that he did anything at once. He just borrowed the key, and pushed off to make a few enquiries, whilst old Barker spent the evening swearing blind *he* didn't know how the key had got there, *he'd* never seen it before, and so on and so forth.

'The more we thought about it the less we liked it. But there was worse to come. Two days later the police were back. They hadn't traced the key, but they'd been making enquiries about those sleeping tablets. And what do you think? They didn't belong to Tania at all. They were Barker's.'

Mr Stoop said, 'Well, what do you know?' and Mr Jopling said, 'Yes, I see,' in the tones of a hanging judge.

'They fairly put Barker through it then. After a bit he admitted buying the tablets. He couldn't deny it, really. They brought along the man who'd sold them to him, to identify him. So why hadn't he said something before?

'He said he'd been scared to say anything about it.

'How had the girl got hold of them? She must have pinched them from his room. What was she doing in his room, anyway? He got deeper and deeper into it. In the end he more or less admitted he'd been intimate with Tania. Of course, he said she led him on.

Which, knowing Tania, was nonsense. However, the one thing he was absolutely firm about was that key. He couldn't think where it had come from. He'd never seen it before.'

'Cold blooded,' said Mr Stoop. 'Make love to her, I take it, then give her a tablet or two to help her off to sleep. Hold her hand until she was well away, turn the gas on, shut the window, and lock the door behind him. He ought to have thrown away the key, though.'

'Strong enough evidence to charge him, I should have thought,' said Mr Jopling. 'I take it they arrested him.'

'Not then and there, they didn't. I think they were still hoping to find the man who'd cut the key for him, and that would have clinched it. But I imagine they left someone watching, to see he didn't get away.'

'Did he try to get away?' said Mr Stoop.

'You might say, in a manner of speaking,' said Mr Burger, 'that he succeeded. Cut his throat, two nights later, in the bathroom.'

In the distance a drum rolled.

The crowd outside raised a cheer.

'Pity they didn't arrest him sooner,' said Mr Jopling.

'A man like that,' said Mr Stoop. 'Hanging would've been too good, in my opinion.'

'In a way, yes,' said Mr Burger. 'In a way, no. Because even that wasn't quite the end of the story. It was about a fortnight later. Joe's last day with us. He was already packed up to go home. We were sitting in the front room waiting for the cab, just him and me. When he pulled out his note case to pay the reckoning a paper came out with it and fell on the floor. I picked it up, and saw it was a receipt for five pounds, in queer sort of writing, with a foreign name on it.

' "Hullo," I say, "what've you been paying out fivers for?"

'He takes it back, looks at it for a moment with a sort of smile on his face, then drops it on the fire.

' "It's not important now," he says, "some money I pay to a comrade. He cut a key for me."

' "He—what?" I say. You know, taking it in slowly. "A key? Are you meaning to tell me—"

' "Nothing," says Joe, "I tell you nothing. Mr Barker, he was responsible for that girl's death. He got her with child. She took her own life."

'I started to say something, but he cut me off pretty sharp.

' "She felt it bad. I think she try twice. Once with the tablets she stole. Not quick enough, perhaps. So she turns the gas on. Don't worry about Mr Barker. He got off lightly.

' "And by the way," he adds, "you'll find all your silver. It's under the coal, in the cellar."

'I was past saying anything by now, and was

275

glad when I heard the cab coming along. Joe gets up and says, very solemn, "If you wish to punish a man, do it with the Law, not against the Law. If you can use the Law for your own ends you can rule the world."

'By this time I'd come to the conclusion that he was either pulling my leg, or he was mad. I said, "Rule the world, eh? Well, just in case you manage to pull it off, Joe, I'd better make a proper note of your name."

'To tell the truth, I'd never seen it written down, and I'd never got my tongue round it since he'd been there.

'"It is no matter," he says, very solemn. "In my country, when a man comes to power, he is born again. He leaves his father's name behind him, and takes a new one from the people."

'I said, to humour him, "I expect you've thought out a nice one for yourself." And so he had.'

The others waited patiently, whilst the noise outside grew. 'Well,' said Mr Jopling, at last. 'What *was* he going to call himself?'

'To tell you the truth,' said Mr Burger. 'It's just slipped my memory. Except that it was a bird. Sparrow, I think. I remember, as he got into the cab, I was pulling his leg about it. "If you and all your friends get into power," I said, "it'll be a regular Parliament of Birds." He didn't seem to think it funny.'

'Foreigners haven't got much sense of

humour,' said Mr Jopling.

'Drink up,' said Mr Stoop. 'Here they come.'

The head of the column was swinging round the corner into their street. A roll of side drums and the shrill squeal of the fifes. Some talk of Alexander, and some of Hercules. Of Hector and Lysander—

They flung open the door. The noise came in like a tidal wave.

Over it Mr Burger was trying to say something.

'Got it,' he shouted.

'Got what?' said Mr Jopling.

'Starling,' said Mr Burger. 'Not sparrow, starling.'

'What's the odds?' Mr Stoop shouted back. 'Sparrow, starling. It isn't cranks like that who are going to rule the world. And they're not going to bother us, neither.'

Outside, the army of the greatest imperial power in the world came marching proudly along the sanded street; marching to usher in a reign of peace and plenty.

THE SEVENTH PARAGRAPH

One feels that some sort of apology is necessary for telling, at this stage, what looks like an escape story, but I can assure you that it is not a PoW story in the accepted sense of the word; and it is certainly one of the oddest things that has ever happened to me.

I was captured by German parachute troops in the early days of the Tunisian campaign, when the front had not settled into its final, muddy, immobility. It was the result of driving over a minefield (probably one laid by our own side), bad map-reading and a measure of bad luck, and that is all that I shall say about that part of it.

I had with me only one signaller and, the front being quiet, our captors had plenty of time to deal with us. I was taken, that night, through a succession of company battalion and Divisional headquarters and finally deposited, very cold and stiff, in an elementary school at Tunis which was being used as a reception camp.

During the course of those successive tramps in the North African starlight, I had successfully extracted from my pocket an operation order, which I shredded and scattered, a marked map, which I squeezed up and dropped into a wadi, and a sheet of paper with wireless 'call signs' and signals on it which, in the best tradition of the Secret Service, I swallowed. There remained only a note book and this I could not easily get at, as it was wedged in the front pocket of my battle dress trousers; and in any event, as far as I could remember, it contained little of importance, being made up of extracts from the printed Field Service Pocket Book (of which the Germans no doubt had already more copies than they knew what to do with). It dealt with such matters as the organisation of supply, the routine for burial of the dead, the disposal of wounded—and, ironically, the disposal of prisoners.

It was only the next morning, when I was summoned to the office of the Camp Commandant and saw among the possessions that had been taken from me, this note book open on the table in front of his interpreter (a man closely resembling and known to all prisoners as Goebbels) that a vague disquiet crept over me. Something to do with the entry about Prisoners of War; some joke.

I squinted anxiously at the book. Although I wear glasses, I have goodish longsight. The page was divided into paragraphs. Paragraph 1 was about getting prisoners back as quickly as possible and paragraph 2 was about not being too friendly with them, in case they got inflated ideas. The next one said 'leave the questioning to Divisional or Corps

Headquarters, who are trained to do it.' Then two paragraphs about administrative matters. Then—good heavens, yes—how could I have forgotten about that. What an idiot I was—in a light hearted mood after Mess one night, on the boat, I had added a private seventh paragraph. There it stood, in all its horrible nakedness. 'Shoot the b—s.' I felt my face going red, and my feet cold. 'We do not quite understand this,' said Goebbels. 'The Commandant wishes to say that he is very angry.'

'Just a joke,' I said.

'He says that he does not understand jokes like that. This is an extract from an official publication?'

'Well, in a way. But of course the last bit isn't in the book.'

'It is an additional instruction added after the book was printed?'

'It isn't an instruction at all.'

'What is it then?'

'Just a joke.'

'It may not prove a joke for you,' said Goebbels.

Nor did it. A miserable time ensued. Goebbels took great pleasure in informing me exactly where I stood. There were rumours already current that the Americans had shot a Tank Crew after it had surrendered; and here, in writing, was evidence of calculated inhumanity at an official level. A policy of frightfulness laid down by Allied Force Headquarters. One which would lead to instant reprisals. Reprisals for which, as Goebbels pointed out, there was one very convenient candidate immediately available.

Late that evening I was taken by car to the German Headquarters in Tunis. The Corps Commander had expressed the desire to see me and cross question me. After waiting in an anteroom for an uncomfortable hour we were told that the Corps Commander was too busy with a battle. He would see me in the morning. I returned to my cell.

This was a former outhouse where, in happier days, perhaps deckchairs and gardening tools had been kept. It was simply furnished with a bale of straw. Also, as I had noticed, the lock was on the inside of the door and attached only by four screws. And Tripoli at that time was no more than 10 miles from the Allied front.

When I reached my cell, I found that I was no longer alone. A South African, in flying kit, was lying disconsolate in the corner. He had been shot down in a Flying Fortress over Biserta that afternoon and was the only survivor. He seemed to have got over his ordeal with considerable resilience and we were soon busy telling each other our life stories.

So naturally selfish is human nature that I can remember nothing of what he told me, except that his name was Ray, but almost everything that I told him. The details of my capture, my experiences of the night before, and above all the terrible predicament that was occupying the forefront of my mind.

'If only,' I said, 'the Germans had a sense of humour.' And later: 'The only solution is to run away. Fortunately that shouldn't be too hard,' and I exposed to him the weakness of the lock.

'Don't rush it,' said Ray. 'You'll want food and water and some sort of map. They let us see the others by day. Maybe we could pick up something from them. We'll have a crack at it together tomorrow night.'

Plans of escape are fatally easy to postpone. We lay down in the straw together and slept. Early next day they came and took Ray away. Air prisoners went to a separate camp. As he left he wished me good luck. I spent the day begging, borrowing and stealing—a bottle of water, some oranges, a tin of meat. Such things were much easier in the slack conditions of a reception centre than they became later.

That evening when I headed for my cell, the German guard shook his head. No more for me my solitary cell. I was to go over to the main block. It had barred windows and a semi-covered door; and a very alert sentry outside it. There was only one consolation. The Corps Commander seemed to have lost interest in me.

All of you will, of course, have arrived at the solution for yourselves. I can only plead that the shock of capture does not conduce to clear thinking. But believe it or not, it was not until weeks later, when I met up with other officers in my unit who had also shared their cell with him, that I even realised that Ray was a stooge, planted on me to gain my confidence.

Well, he gained it all right. I cannot remember that I gave him any military information. I was far too interested in my own fate to worry about the rest of the Army. And I apparently convinced him of my innocence. So maybe he did me a good turn.

SUPERINTENDENT MAHOOD AND THE CRAVEN CASE

It was a lovely morning in late September. The sun was shining, and Superintendent Mahood, who was off duty for the weekend, had just finished a leisurely breakfast, and was on the point of lighting his pipe, when the doorbell of his flat sounded.

Had it turned out to be anyone else but Mr Spalling, the Superintendent might have been rude. There were a lot of good reasons for not being rude to Mr Spalling, senior partner in the firm of Spalling, Lampeter and Fosdyke, solicitors, of King's Bench Walk. First, because he was a friend of the Assistant Commissioner; but more than that, because they had worked together on many a black market case, in the days at the end of the war, when Mahood was a junior Inspector, and Mr Spalling was in the legal department of the Board of Trade; and he had learnt to appreciate the solicitor as a meticulously accurate, imperturbable old body, equally unlikely to panic or to exaggerate.

He was all the more impressed, therefore, when Mr Spalling opened the conversation by saying, 'The A-C sent me along to have a word with you. Somebody's trying to murder one of my clients.'

'Help yourself to coffee,' said Mahood, 'and tell me about it.'

'It's a girl of twenty,' said Mr Spalling. 'Domina Craven. She's the only daughter of the late Sam Craven.'

'Theatre owner. Impressario. Millionaire.'

'That's him. I'd better give you the legal picture first. Sam left all his money to his daughter. The widow gets an annuity.'

'Lucky daughter.'

'She *will* be lucky,' said Mr Spalling. 'If she gets it. She has to come of age first. That happy event takes place this Wednesday. If she doesn't reach the age of twenty-one, it goes to Domina's cousin, Monica, for life. She's a month or two younger than Domina. On *her* death it goes to theatrical charities.'

'And why,' said the Superintendent, 'should we suppose that a young lady of twenty is going to die?'

'About six months ago,' said Mr Spalling, 'Domina started getting anonymous letters. She thought the first one was a joke, and she sent it to me.' He extracted a letter and an envelope from his briefcase and laid them on the table.

'Vague,' said the Superintendent. 'But threatening.'

'The others were worse, I gather. I haven't been allowed to see them. She destroyed them. It can't be nice to know that someone in your own family circle wants you dead.'

285

'Family circle?'

'So she says. The letters were full of family allusions. And hints. All harping, rather nastily, on the fate which is going to overtake her before she comes of age. She's a highly strung girl. All of old Sam's artistic temperament, without his essential ballast. Too much money, and a stupid mother.'

The Superintendent read the letter again, examined the envelope, and said: 'Did *you* take it seriously?'

Mr Spalling said, with a wintry smile, 'There's a million pounds involved. I always take a million pounds seriously. I asked the local Chief Constable, who's an old friend of mine, to help. He got one of his retired police sergeants—a good man called Prater—taken on as gardener. You'll find him a great help when you go down to Great Willing.'

'So I'm going down, am I?'

'I much hope you'll do so,' said Mr Spalling, 'and stay there until Wednesday, when Domina comes of age. The Assistant Commissioner hopes so too.'

'Hmmm,' said Mahood. 'Who else is in the house?'

'Apart from Domina, her mother, and cousin Monica, you'll find Martin Sherry, who's engaged to Monica, and a Major Flemish, who would like, I gather, to be engaged to Mrs Craven. I had some impertinent letters from him earlier in the year, suggesting I ought to let Mrs Craven have a bit of capital and he once had the impertinence to try to engage me in conversation on the subject. I was forced to point out to him that it was contrary to Rule 23 of our Club rules to discuss any form of business in the Smoking Room.'

'What are the others like?'

'I've never met them,' said Mr Spalling. 'Nor have I been to Great Willing. Like most solicitors—though unlike policemen—I believe that the place to do my business is in my office.'

'Grrh!' said Mahood.

As soon as Mr Spalling had departed, Mahood had a word on the telephone with the Assistant Commissioner.

'I'm glad you could go,' said the A.C. 'Unofficially, of course. I gather you'll be introduced as a business friend of the old boy's. I'll send Norcutt with you.'

Mahood remembered Sergeant Norcutt, a co-operative person, who had earned a lot of good marks in the recent Lewisham anonymous letter case.

'Fine,' he said. 'I'll park the Sergeant in the village pub to pick up gossip.'

* * *

Eleven o'clock was striking from the clock above the stable courtyard when Mahood turned his old Morris into the gate of Great Willing.

The driveway ran through an area of woodland, a tame wilderness, with symmetrical glades and carefully organized prospects. He stopped to admire; and was startled to see, at the end of one of the rides, a totally unclad nymph standing on her head.

On closer inspection he realized that it was an illusion. A white marble figure had been placed beside a clear basin of water. A carefully positioned spray of foliage hid her from view, leaving only her reflection visible.

Mahood thought he detected the fine hand of the late Sam Craven in the arrangement. He restarted his car, and drove slowly on, past the walled kitchen garden. Here he braked again, at the sight of a man hoeing.

The sound brought the man's head round; and when he saw Mahood, he straightened his back, propped his hoe carefully against his wheelbarrow, and walked across to the car.

'Sergeant Prater?'

'Mr Prater now,' said the man.

'Superintendent Mahood, from Central.'

'They told me someone was coming,' said Prater. 'Not before it was time, either.'

'Bad as that, is it?' said Mahood.

'I tell you,' said Prater, 'every time I come past that lake, I wonder if I won't have to pick her out. This letter writing. It's driving her off her head. She can't hardly bear to see the

288

postman come up to the house.'

'Not much longer now,' said Mahood. 'If anything is to happen, it'll be in the next few days. If there's any trouble, I'd like to know how I can get hold of you quickly.'

'I've got a flat over the stable. It used to be the head gardener's. Four gardeners they had. I do it all now, with an odd job man.'

'Transport?'

'I've got a motor bike. There's no buses out here. You'd hardly think London was only thirty miles away, would you?'

Mahood agreed. It was an enchanting spot, even if it had run a bit wild since Sam Craven's death. The house he judged to be about eighty years old. A solid, two-storey brick and stone building with no nonsense about it.

His hand was raised to ring the bell, when the front door opened and a middle-aged, military-looking gentleman stepped out.

'Hullo,' he said. 'And who are you?'

'I'm Mahood.'

'Ah—yes. My name's Flemish. You're the chap who's come to sell Domina a theatre, aren't you? She said something about you.'

'Not exactly,' said Mahood. 'As a matter of fact, I—' He broke off.

At the far end of the short hallway, a girl was standing, pressed against the wall, out of sight, but clearly reflected in the mirror.

Major Flemish said, 'I see you've spotted

her. Don't worry. There's no one there. It's a picture on the opposite wall. One of Sam's tricks. This house is full of things like that.'

His blue, protuberant eyes looked Mahood up and down. There was intelligence in them, and spite. Not a very likeable man. But not a man to be underrated.

'Lombard'll see to your bag,' he said. 'He's about somewhere. I've just got to telephone my bookmaker. I've been put on to a nag for the three o'clock at Brighton.' He consulted the paper in his hand. 'Are you a racing man?'

'Only greyhounds,' said Mahood.

When Lombard, the portly butler, had shown him his room, Mahood wandered down. The house was very silent.

He tried a door on the south side of the hall. It opened into as pleasant a room as he could remember seeing. Along the whole of one side deeply embrasured windows gave on to a loggia. Between the embrasures were low, built-in bookcases of white wood, on which stood bowls of roses.

A slight sound brought his head round. A girl was seated, hidden almost, in a high backed chair, watching him. He was conscious of a pair of worried eyes, set in a white face which contrasted strangely with a mop of reddish hair. It was a sensitive face, a face which felt things. The face, he thought, of a girl not very well equipped to deal with the problems of life, but who might make

290

something of them if she got the right sort of help.

'You must be my watch dog,' she said. 'I'm Domina. You don't look much like a policeman.'

'What do policemen look like?'

'Horrible. They always wear raincoats—even when the sun is shining. And keep their hats on in the house.'

'You've been seeing too many films,' said Mahood. 'And I don't believe that even the most hardened policeman would keep his hat on in a room like this.'

'Willing is a nice place,' said Domina. 'Only it's full of ghosts.'

'Ghosts?'

'Ghosts of my father and his peculiar sense of humour.'

'You mean things like the nymph standing on her head by the lake? And the young lady eavesdropping in the hall?'

'There's even a trick mirror in here.' Domina got up and moved across to the window embrasure. 'If I sit in the chair—just here—between these two windows, and you're standing on the terrace, you can't see me, but you can see my reflection in that long mirror by the fireplace. It spoils that wall, I think.'

'Your father,' said Mahood, 'must have been rather an odd man.'

'He was a great big baby,' said Domina, 'and we all loved him. We miss him dreadfully, you know. Mother in particular. I'm only praying she doesn't miss him *too* much.'

Mahood looked up. 'You mean the military gentleman?'

'I mean Major Flemish,' agreed Domina. 'He's an old friend of the family. I'd much prefer him to stay that way. I don't want him as a step-father.'

'Does he want you as a step-daughter?'

She managed to smile. 'That's not a very gallant question. Now—shall I tell you about the others?'

'I'll be meeting them,' said Mahood. 'Tell me, first, about the letters.'

'I'd much rather not.'

'As bad as that, were they?'

She thought for some time, before saying: 'Do you know what it's like to have someone making fun of you, but in a cold, cruel way?'

Mahood said, 'It can happen. The real trouble is when you can't get away from it. At school, I mean. Or at work. Usually, when you're grown up, you can avoid people like that.'

'It's utterly and unspeakably loathsome,' said Domina. 'It goes on and on. I burn every letter I get. If I'd an ounce more courage, I wouldn't open them at all. And the person who writes them knows that—'

'Domina, darling,' said a voice from the doorway, and Mrs Craven swept in. Mahood got up. 'This is Mr Mahood,' said Domina.

'Lovely to see you,' said Mrs Craven. 'Isn't it a beautiful day. You must get Domina to show you the garden. There's just time before luncheon.'

At lunch he met the two other members of the household. Monica was a pleasant, obviously intelligent girl, with a touch of masculine hardness in her face; Martin Sherry he put down as an ageing Peter Pan.

After lunch, Mahood found himself drinking his coffee alone with Monica. As soon as Lombard had closed the door she said, 'I suppose you're some sort of policeman.'

'Never has any deception deceived so few people,' said Mahood. 'Yes. I'm a policeman.'

'Keeping an eye on Domina?'

'That's right.'

'You'll have to put up with us till she comes of age. Incidentally, when does that happen?'

'Her mother informs me,' said Mahood, carefully, 'that Domina was born at the precise moment that the curtain fell on the first night of her husband's big Ice Revue. "Polar Bares," I understand, was its name. She confirmed this by showing me a telegram he sent her, from the theatre, which ran "Hope your first production is as successful as mine."'

Monica said, unsmiling, 'But you don't come of age at the moment you're born, surely. It's the first minute after midnight—

isn't that right?'

'I'm not sure,' said Mahood. 'Or do you have to last out the whole of your birthday? I must find out.' He got up.

'Ask Martin,' said Monica. '*He* knows all the answers.'

Mahood detected a note of reserve in her voice. 'Your fiancé?'

'My fiancé,' agreed Monica. 'A man who loves no one but himself. You've heard about marriages of convenience? That's what this one's going to be. His convenience, of course.'

Mahood looked at her curiously. 'You must excuse an impertinent question,' he said. 'But aren't you in love with him?'

The hard grey eyes looked back into his. 'Love's an illusion,' said Monica. 'Like most other things in this house.'

It was later on that afternoon, as Mahood was making his way up to his own bedroom to finish unpacking, that he heard his name called, and opening the door on the other side of the landing, found Martin Sherry sprawled in an easy chair, in what was evidently his private bed-sitting room.

'I thought I recognized those number twelve boots,' said Martin. 'You *are* a policeman, aren't you?'

'Well—yes, actually I am,' said Mahood resignedly. 'How *did* you guess?'

'Pretty obvious, really,' said Martin. 'Someone's got to see the filly past the

294

winning post. Have a drink. I've just rung for Lombard.' He pointed, with one elegant toe to a bell-push on the foot rest. 'Ingenious, isn't it? Everything I need. Chair, foot rest, book rest, reading light . . .'

'It looks very comfortable,' said Mahood.

'Oh, I'm pretty well dug in here. I've been here nearly six years altogether. They're a nice family. I'm meant to be marrying Monica, did you know?'

'I gathered that you were engaged.'

'I've never really been able to make out,' said Martin, shifting to a slightly more convenient position in his chair, 'what the idea of people getting married is. Bit more permanent, I suppose. Freehold instead of leasehold, if you follow me. Oh, Lombard, thank you. What about a drink for you, Mahood? Sure you won't? That's all for the moment then, Lombard.'

'Did you make all these gadgets yourself?' asked Mahood, gazing round the curiously cluttered room.

'Surely. I'm a professional gadgeteer. That's how I first met old Craven. He worked out his jokes. I constructed 'em. He was a great man for jokes.'

'Trick mirrors you mean? Like the ones in the hall and the drawing-room.'

'The house is full of that sort of thing,' said Martin. 'He asked a covey of magicians to dinner once, and halfway through the fish course a whacking great chandelier over the table broke loose and crashed on top of them. Or seemed to. All done by mirrors. You ought to have seen the guests scatter. The old boy laughed so much he nearly broke a blood vessel.'

'A curiously child-like sense of humour.'

'You've said it. And talking of retarded mentalities, watch out for the Major. You know he's after the widow.'

'So Miss Craven implied, yes.'

'A dangerous man. He keeps a regular arsenal in his room. Last war relics. Two pistols at least, and a box of grenades.'

'How on earth do you know?'

'Oh, I happened to be in his room one day,' said Martin. 'I wanted to borrow a handkerchief and I opened one of his drawers—'

Mahood was first down to tea, and found time for a word with Lombard.

'I hope you find everything to your liking, sir.'

'Very much so, thank you,' said Mahood. 'Have you been with the family long, Lombard?'

'Thirty years, sir. I came as footman. We had an indoor staff of seven in those days.'

'No one's got much money nowadays,' said Mahood. 'It's death duties.'

'That's what it will be, I imagine,' said Lombard. 'It's only myself and Mrs

Grumbridge now. Would you care for anchovy toast?' For a time no one else appeared, and Mahood had resigned himself to a solitary tea when the door opened and Domina came in.

'I'm afraid the tea's a bit cold—' he began, then realized she was not listening. Her attention was outside the room.

In the distance, the front door-bell shrilled.

'It's the postman,' she said. 'He always comes about now. I do hope—this time—' She broke off, and they waited in awkward silence until Lombard reappeared. In his hand he had a salver, and on it a single letter.

From where he sat, Mahood could see that the envelope was typewritten, and had an express letter stamp on it.

With a savage effort of self-control Domina waited until Lombard had withdrawn, before splitting open the envelope. There was silence as she read it. Then, in a shaky voice, she said: 'It *is* another letter. But it doesn't seem to be quite as bad as some of them. I can't make it out.'

It was typewritten on a sheet of white quarto paper, and it said:

'*Don't cut your corners. Concentrate on cyanide. Play fair. And the person to watch is L.N.S.P.C.I.*'

'What is it?' she said. 'A sort of code?'

'Something of the sort,' said Mahood. He seemed to be more interested in the envelope

297

than the letter. 'Will Lombard keep his mouth shut?'

'Yes.'

'I'll hang on to this, if I may. Don't mention it to anyone. Do you know, I really think we may be getting somewhere at last.'

He smiled at Domina, who managed to smile back.

*　　*　　*

Mahood spent the evening in his room, scribbling out a preliminary report. After supper he strolled down to the pub, where he found Sergeant Norcutt playing darts in the bar.

'I'm pretty certain,' he said, 'that I know who the nigger in *this* woodpile is. I want you to take a report to the A-C first thing in the morning. It'll be Sunday, but Central will be able to locate him for you. Next thing—have a word with Spalling and find out *when* a person comes of age. Is it the moment they were born, or the midnight before, or when is it? Then get round to Major Flemish's digs. Have a word with his landlady. Also his club.' 'What are we after, sir?'

'I want to know all about the Major's letter writing habits. Whether he uses a typewriter. If he's a prolific letter writer—or only an occasional one. How much mail he receives. And any background material about his character and habits. In fact, you've got quite a day's work.'

'You're telling me,' said the Sergeant.

*   *   *

An extract from Sergeant Norcutt's report, delivered verbally to the Superintendent behind the stables at six o'clock on Sunday evening, subsequently written out, and forming part of the dossier on the Craven case:

'His landlady said she had never known the Major post a letter, or ask her to post a letter. She thought he did all that sort of thing at his Club. She thought him a pleasant enough gentleman, a little childish sometimes. He paid his rent regularly and was no trouble. The under-porter at the Club was more helpful. I gathered the impression that he did not much like the Major. He allowed me to see his room. There is a typewriter there, on which I typed the attached few lines. The porter told me that the Major was very methodical about letters. Made a note of every one he sent or received. "A regular old maid" he described him as. I noticed a number of war relics, including a box of grenade fuses. I contacted the A-C who was spending the weekend with Mr Spalling. Mr Spalling says that Miss Craven will come of age legally one minute after midnight on

299

Tuesday night. That is to say, on the first minute of the Wednesday morning. They both wished you good luck.'

'Decent of them,' said Mahood. He was scrutinising the typewritten sample. There was no shadow of doubt in his mind. The letter which had arrived at teatime the previous day had been typed on the same machine. It was high time for a showdown.

He summoned Prater from his cottage, introduced Sergeant Norcutt to him, and gave certain instructions.

'It's possible,' he said, 'that Major Flemish may try to do a bunk. That old Bentley belongs to him doesn't it?'

'That's right,' said Prater. 'There's no room for it in the coach house, so he keeps it out here.'

'If he tries to leave, could you keep up with him on your motor cycle?'

'There isn't a car on the road can lose me,' said Prater with a grin.

Mahood went off to look for the Major, and found him in his room, dismantling a Luger.

'Sit down, sit down,' said the Major. 'Martin tells me you're a detective. Have you located our letter writer yet?'

'Yes,' said Mahood. 'I have. Just *why* did you send that silly letter to Miss Craven? The one you posted, express, in London yesterday morning.'

The Major seemed unabashed.

300

'Everyone seemed to be getting a bit worked up about things,' he said. 'I thought a bit of humour might liven things up.'

'You thought it a joke to send a letter which made a direct accusation against another member of the household?'

'You worked that out, did you?' said the Major. 'When I was in the "I" Corps I dabbled around with cyphers. Ingenious don't you think.'

'I think it was childish, vindictive and unnecessary,' said Mahood. 'I suppose you typed it at your club—where you write all your letters.'

'I say, you *have* been snooping around, haven't you? Yes. I write all my letters there. I don't type 'em all. Only type business letters. I think this modern habit of typing personal letters—'

'And did you type all the other anonymous letters there?'

This time the Major really did look surprised.

'You're way off beam, old boy,' he said. 'I didn't type the other letters.'

'In that case,' said Mahood, 'perhaps you'll explain how both this envelope'—he laid on the table the envelope in which the first letter, which Mr Spalling had handed to him, had come—'and the one that arrived yesterday have both got such curious similarities. Look at the capital K's and capital Ws.' The Major's face had suddenly turned livid. 'Or are you suggesting,' went on Mahood, 'that the similarities are a coincidence?'

'I'm suggesting—' said the Major, and broke off. 'Are you charging me with something?'

'Not yet.'

'Then I'm suggesting you leave my room.'

'We've got him on the move,' said Mahood to Prater, with whom he had a word before he went to bed. 'Better watch out first thing tomorrow. If he's going to bunk, he'll do it good and early.'

*   *   *

It was half past six on the following morning, and just light, when the Major emerged.

Mahood, who was sitting beside his bedroom window, fully dressed, picked up the house telephone and spoke to Prater, who seemed to be awake also.

'He's coming,' he said. 'Give him a hundred yards. Telephone me here when you've found out where he's going.'

'If he's off for good,' said Prater, who was evidently also at his window, 'why hasn't he got a bag with him?'

'Search me,' said Mahood. 'He's—God in heaven!'

In front of their eyes, the old Bentley erupted. First a flash of white flame, then a muffled explosion from inside the car; then a drift of grey-white smoke curled through the shattered windscreen.

Nearly three hours later, things were under some sort of control. The local police had taken charge. Everyone in the house had been questioned and everyone had simply said that they had gone to bed at the usual time the night before, and had been woken by the explosion.

A first examination of the car had shown that some sort of bomb or grenade had been placed under the bonnet, connected, it seemed likely, with the activating arm of the self-starter. A search of the Major's room had revealed a sack of Mills grenades and a box of loose primers.

It was difficult to say if one had been taken out or not. It also revealed the Major's washing and shaving tackle, fresh used; which seemed to indicate that his early morning departure had not been intended to be permanent.

Mahood found time for a word with Prater, who had stolidly resumed his gardener's duties.

'Never heard a sound,' he said. 'But it's quite likely I wouldn't. I'm a heavy sleeper.'

'I'm usually a very light sleeper,' said Mahood, 'and I should have expected to hear if anyone had left—hullo?'

He bent forward and examined a pea-stick which had been planted to mark the end of a line of Prater's planting. There were similar sticks ranged behind it, each cleft at the top and holding an empty seed packet.

'I put 'em in to mark what's planted,' said Prater. 'What—?'

He too bent forward.

'Rather a curious form of autumn vegetable,' said Mahood softly. He extracted the envelope from the stick, and holding it firmly by one corner, slipped in the blade of his penknife, and slit it open.

'*How good are your nerves?*' said the typewritten message. '*How are you going to last out Monday and Tuesday? Hadn't you better take the quick way out—as your friend the Major has?*'

The envelope was addressed simply: '*Miss Domina Craven. By hand,*' and below that, '*Final Demand.*'

'You'll give it to her?' said Prater.

'Would you?' said Mahood.

Prater looked surprised. 'I don't know. It's addressed to her. I suppose I should've.'

'Then it's lucky I found it and not *you,*' said Mahood, 'because I'm not going to show it to her at all.'

He walked back to the house, conscious that Prater was staring after him.

*   *   *

To say that the rest of the household was

shaken by the sudden death of the Major would be a gross understatement. For the moment, all the spirit seemed to have gone out of them. They offered no opposition when Mahood—who introduced himself to them in his official capacity for the first time—warned them that none of them must leave the house until he gave them permission.

Lunch and tea were taken almost in silence. The demoralisation seemed to have spread to Lombard and the unseen Mrs Grumbridge, for dinner, which should have been at half past eight, was nearly an hour late, and took an hour and a half to serve.

It was a dispirited little party who gathered in the drawing room afterwards.

Here, however, for the first time that day, tongues were loosened, and, under the stimulus of a special bottle of liqueur brandy which Lombard was inspired to bring in with the coffee, discussion began in earnest.

'How *could* anyone,' said Mrs Craven, for the seventh time, 'how *could* anyone have been so cold-blooded and heartless—and to choose for their victim such an inoffensive person as the Major, whom we have all known and admired all our lives.'

Martin, lounging in the window seat, may have felt that this was going a bit too far, even as a eulogy of the recently dead, and had opened his mouth to protest, when Superintendent Mahood came in.

305

All eyes swung towards him. It was clear that he had something of moment to announce.

'I am sorry,' he said, 'to have kept you under such strict house arrest. You will have to take my word for it that it was necessary. The menace which threatens all of us—of the reality of which we had such grim warning this morning—may strike again, and quite soon.'

Mrs Craven looked with apprehension at the undrawn curtains, and Mahood caught the gesture, and interpreted it correctly.

'I asked Lombard to leave the curtains undrawn,' he said. 'It may seem to increase the danger of attack, but in fact, the reverse is true. You would all agree, I think, that it is better that this hidden menace should be brought into the open. Otherwise, who knows how long it may lurk and threaten.'

There was a murmur of agreement.

'I have spent the time since dinner,' went on Mahood, 'making certain preparations. First'—and he went to the door and opened it—'I have asked Sergeant Norcutt, who has been down in the village, to come up and help me. A situation may develop any moment now, when two pairs of eyes are better than one.'

Sergeant Norcutt smiled amiably at the company, then looked back quickly at the Superintendent. It was evident that the Sergeant, like everyone else present, sensed the mounting tension.

'Next,' said Mahood. 'I must make a request of Miss Craven. I want her to move her chair back, into the embrasure between these two windows, and turn it slightly to the left. That's right. A little more, please, and an inch forward.'

He arranged her with the minute care of a photographer arranging a sitter, then moved across the room until he had his back against the left hand of the two windows overlooking the dark terrace. From where he stood, the illusion was nearly perfect. To someone outside, it would have been quite perfect.

The real Domina was tucked away out of sight, in the window embrasure. Her reflection appeared in the unframed mirror, cunningly angled and set between two bookcases on the opposite wall.

Mahood returned to his station by the door, and cast a final eye over the scene, as anxiously as any stage manager at a moment before curtain rise.

'If you could give us the faintest idea of what all this is about,' said Monica. She seemed the calmest of them all.

'How long have we got to keep this up?' asked Martin.

'Any moment now,' said Mahood. And the words were scarcely out of his mouth when it happened. A sharp crack, as of a whip. A tinkle of broken window glass. And in front of their eyes, the mirror on the left of the fireplace starred and disintegrated as the bullet hit it.

Mahood's hands flew to the switch, and the room was in darkness. They heard him fumbling with the window curtains, and a sharp, 'Give me a hand, Sergeant!'

Then the lights came on again.

Domina, her mother, Monica and Martin were all sitting, frozen to their chairs, their frightened eyes fixed on the Superintendent. Martin recovered his voice first.

'You're letting him get away,' he squeaked.

'Who's getting away?'

'The murderer—out there—in the garden.'

'This house has been surrounded by policemen since dusk,' said Mahood. 'No one's getting away. Inside or outside.' He surveyed the people in the room with grim satisfaction and added, 'Of course, it's quite clear now who's been writing these silly letters, and killed Major Flemish—and tried to kill Miss Craven . . .'

*   *   *

The reader was then told to assume that the same person (let's call them X) wrote all the anonymous letters (other than the Major's 'joke' letter), killed the Major and was responsible for the shot fired into the room. The author says that there are nine or ten

308

clues in the story all pointing to one person.

The questions you should now ask yourself are:

(a) Who was X?
(b) What was X's motive for the anonymous letter campaign?
(c) How does Mahood *know* that the letters must have been written by X and no one else?
(d) Why did X have to kill the Major?
(e) How did X arrange the killing?
(f) Why did X risk such a public shot at Domina? Or was it a blind?

Solution

Published in Suspense October 1959

(a) The solicitor, Mr Spalling is X.
(b) Spalling is the trustee of Domina's money which he has appropriated. When Domina dies, it will go to Monica for life but he will remain the trustee. Spalling hopes to use the letter campaign to push Domina to suicide.
(c) The letters must have been written by somebody with a close knowledge of Domina, which Spalling had. Mr Spalling is also a member of the Major's club and would therefore have access to

his typewriter.

(d)   The Major realised that the letter had been typed using his typewriter and that Spalling had access to it as a member of the same club. He then made the mistake of trying to blackmail Spalling. Spalling killed him to keep him quiet.

(e)   Spalling requested the Major to drive over early to meet him the following morning. The fuse and grenade used for the killing came from the cache at the Major's club.

(f)   Domina reaches her majority on Tuesday morning, not Wednesday (we have only Spalling's say-so for the Wednesday). The murder attempt takes place after 11 p.m. on Monday night and this is therefore the last possible time for her demise.

The shot was fired by someone who did not know of the existence of the trick mirror. Of all the people who were close to Domina, this is probably Spalling.

ARNOLD OR THE USES OF ELECTRICITY

Girls and boys—sisters and brothers—
Are supposed to love their mothers.
It's hard to tell. It may be so,
Girls are deceptive; but I know
That there are many boys who'd rather
Carry on without a father.
For fathers take the dimmest view
Of almost all a boy can do,
And demonstrate this hostile feeling
With stern rebukes. Nay, sometimes dealing
Harsh punishments which they design
To keep their errant sons in line.
How often does some harmless act
Result in sonny getting smacked.
All boys dislike a hit upon
Their tender little sit-upon.
None more than Arnold who, poor lad,
Appeared to drive his father mad
A curious response to meet
From one who'd much to keep him sweet.
Vintage burgundies in bins,
Substantial balances at Glynns,
Servants, a chauffeur and a wife
Who led a self-denying life.
A London house, a model farm,
Surely enough to keep him calm
Thought Arnold, who had strong objection

311

To undeserved (he held) correction.

Now Arnold's teachers did not find
Young Arnold such a constant bind.
In all his school reports are found
'Good' or 'Exceptionally sound'.
No boy got higher marks than he
In physics and in chemistry.
Of Science ('Theory' and 'Applied')
His knowledge was both deep and wide.
Did he confine his studies to
Those taught at school? No, sir, he knew
That private study is the way
A boy gets on. That very day
He'd built a workshop in the attic
To watch the thrilling—if erratic—
Conduct of volts and amps and ohms
With which, as are all modern homes,
His house was furnished. Here, it seems,
Lay the seed of Arnold's dreams.
He was, of course, full well aware
Of all the thought and boundless care
For prudence and security
Imported by the G.E.C.
The cut-outs, fuses and devices,
Safeguards against domestic crisis.
But logic and analysis
Can side-step obstacles like this.
The safest fuses yet invented
Could be quite simply circumvented,
If you removed the fuse wire, and
Replaced it with a thicker brand

Of wire. A hairpin would, he knew
Allow the strongest current through.
He next affixed an extra wire
Inside the bell beside the fire
In his father's writing room,
Then waited for the certain doom
Of his papa. He thought, with glee,
That's the answer! Q.E.D.

But in this life the wise man knows
That 'homme propose' but 'Dieu dispose'.
Instead of all that high-tec stuff,
Physics and scientific guff,
Had he but happened to traverse
The Oxford Book of English Verse
He would have found the place where Burns
Warns that the craftiest concerns
Of mice and men gang aft agley
And so it chanced. The following day
Arnold was ordered to appear
In his father's study, where
He faced a merited reproof
For climbing on the stable roof.
On this occasion dad, though sore
Was too exhausted to do more
Than utter verbal castigation.
And, rounding off this exhortation,
Said to Arnold, 'Fetch the maid.
I need strong drink. My nerves are frayed.'
When Arnold hesitated, he
Added, in tones of contumely
'They say you're brainy. Bloody hell.

Don't you know how to ring a bell?'
And pouncing like a savage lion
Upon his pale and trembling scion
Dragged him across the carpet, and
Seizing his unresisting hand
Pressed it upon the fatal button;
Killing them both as dead as mutton.

At one fell swoop young Arnold's mum
Becomes a matrimonial plum.
With lots of cash, and unencumbered
By a tiresome son she's numbered
Among the most exclusive batches
Of that season's marriage catches.
She very quickly caught the eye
Of poor, but noble, Lord de Wye
Who married her without delay
And whisked her off to Wyeville Tay
A noble mansion in the west
There she could entertain the best
Of all the County's personnel;
And, goodness, did she do them well!
Her friends all said, 'My dear, it's great.
But is it really up-to-date?
Your lamps are oil; your fires are wood
Might it be better if you could
Modernise just a little more.
The electric grid is at your door.'

But Arnold's mum was firm. She knew
What electricity could do.

APPENDIX

Game Without Rules, a series in twenty parts

In Which Mr Calder Acquires a Dog (published as 'Emergency Exit')	28 October 1968
The Peaceful People	31 October 1968
The Spoilers	4 & 7 November 1968
The Road to Damascus	11 November 1968
Cat Cracker	14 November 1968
Double, Double	18 & 21 November 1968
One-to-Ten	25 November 1968
The African Tree Beavers	28 November 1968
Cross-Over	2 & 5 December 1968
The Lion and the Virgin	9 December 1968
Ahmed and Ego (published as 'The Decline and Fall of Mr Behrens')	12 December 1968
The Mercenaries	16 December 1968
Churchill's Men	19 December 1968
Heilige Nacht	23 & 26 December 1968
Signal Tresham	30 December 1968
St Ethelburga and the Angel of Death	2 January 1969